FIGHT
NO MORE

FIGHT
NO MORE

stories

LYDIA
MILLET

W. W. NORTON & COMPANY

Independent Publishers Since 1923

New York | London

Fight No More is a work of fiction. Names, characters, places, and incidents are the products of the author's imagination or are used fictitiously. Any resemblance to actual events, locales, or persons, living or dead, is entirely coincidental.

Many thanks to my friends David Hancocks, Susie Deconcini, Matthew Silverman, and Aaron Young for their help on the details of these fictions, as well as to my dear agent Maria Massie, my editor Tom Mayer, and my publicist Elizabeth Riley. I'm grateful to Lauren Abbate, Sarah Bolling, Steve Colca, Dan Christiaens, Julia Druskin, Emma Hitchcock, Rebecca Homiski, Francine Kass, Ingsu Liu, Dave Mallman, Meredith McGinnis, Joe Murphy, Steven Pace, Golda Rademacher, Karen Rice, Don Rifkin, and Nomi Victor at Norton, and to my wonderful copy editor Amy Robbins, for all they did to make this book.

For information about permission to reproduce selections from this book, write to Permissions, W. W. Norton & Company, Inc., 500 Fifth Avenue, New York, NY 10110

For information about special discounts for bulk purchases, please contact W. W. Norton Special Sales at specialsales@wwnorton.com or 800-233-4830

Manufacturing by Quad Graphics Fairfield
Book design by Chris Welch
Production manager: Lauren Abbate

Library of Congress Cataloging-in-Publication Data

Names: Millet, Lydia, 1968– author.
Title: Fight no more : stories / Lydia Millet.
Description: First Edition. | New York : W. W. Norton & Company, [2018]
Identifiers: LCCN 2017054853 | ISBN 9780393635485 (hardcover)
Classification: LCC PS3563.I42175 A6 2018 | DDC 813/.54—dc23
LC record available at https://lccn.loc.gov/2017054853

W. W. Norton & Company, Inc., 500 Fifth Avenue, New York, N.Y. 10110
www.wwnorton.com

W. W. Norton & Company Ltd., 15 Carlisle Street, London W1D 3BS

1 2 3 4 5 6 7 8 9 0

CONTENTS

FIGHT
NO MORE

LIBERTINES

She stood for a moment in the quiet bathroom, in its stillness that was like a held breath. Then she opened the book, sat down on the toilet and let a line of type catch her eye.

"Supper and the orgies transpired without unusual incident."

Disappointing: a page without graphic sex. She only had a couple of minutes till the showing, though, so she closed the book and swiveled it back into position on the shelf over the bidet. Not the first time she'd hid out in a bathroom all furtive: when she was a kid, the neighbors two doors down had kept a copy of *The Joy of Sex* in a basket beside their toilet. They had an orange shag rug on their toilet lid. The book featured line drawings of naked old people with nests of curly hair around their private parts; seeing those pictures, her little sister screamed.

After they discovered it, the two of them used to find any excuse to go pee in that house. Sometimes they'd claimed their own toilet was clogged.

Later, when they were in their twenties, her sister denounced the book at someone's bridal shower. "Groovy sex is worse than no sex at all," she had said. That was before she stopped drinking and turned to self-help.

In this book, musty with age, there were no pictures. Just many, many words. Too many. In general she didn't read long books, but for porn she was willing to make an exception. This porn used old-fashioned language—a buzzkill when she first found the book, but it grew on her over time. French dukes lined up dozens of kidnapped virgins and proceeded to "deflower" them. At first, in her mind's eye, there had been literal flowers. A damsel held them up in a small bouquet until a duke came running at her, punched her, then grabbed the bouquet and stamped on it.

Luckily the owners didn't care what people thought of them, or she'd never have seen the book. But this was an old-money house, and old money didn't give a shit. New money tended to stash its porn in drawers. Even safes. She'd seen it: safes. Unless the new money was a creative, and then all bets were off. One actress whose house she'd sold had a purple sculpture on her coffee table of a guy with his head between a woman's spread legs.

"*Jeff Eating Ilona*," the actress had proudly told her was its title. "A limited edition."

Gate buzzer. She headed downstairs, checking herself in a hall mirror. She'd emailed this client a few houses but he hadn't liked any of them; this was the only property he wanted to see. He'd come into the office briefly with his driver, and someone had whispered that he was an African leader; he wore a hat of spotted fur. It made you think of corruption, maybe a coup or child soldiers . . . but this wasn't going to be the house for him either. The view was breathtaking on clear days, but the place wasn't modern enough. Powerful men wanted their houses shiny.

He'd have to fall into the new-rich category, as a dictator, she thought, because a dictator didn't act like old money. She'd read about one recently who showed off on his birthday by eating a baby elephant. Old money, well, maybe they'd eat an aging elephant, maybe an elephant that was already sick, if it was on offer at a dinner party. Maybe. They wouldn't care to be rude. Most often, though, fine-dining-wise, they'd steer clear of an elephant.

She didn't know for a fact that he was a dictator, obviously. She did know he was standoffish. His assistant, or whoever had called to make the original appointment, had said not to address him directly. It might be a religious thing. She'd recently had a sheikh like that: Saudi. The sheikh's handlers asked her to avert her eyes whenever she talked to him because he didn't like to be looked at by a Western woman. Such women were harlots, sadly.

She smiled as she pushed the button to open the gate. There were harlots in the book, but she acted nothing like them.

Too bad.

The sheikh would only consider reinforced masonry—he'd wanted to buy a house for his daughter, who was a freshman at USC—but nothing had been good enough, plus the whole family hated every neighborhood. Only Bel Air they liked, but the daughter finally said no to the house there, near the country club, claiming it was depressing. Also the smell in the four-car garage was "weird." (Mothballs.) Had the person who lived in the house died?

Well yes, in fact, she'd wanted to say, because that's the only way anyone *ever* leaves a house this stunning. Of course she hadn't admitted it. Buyers didn't like houses where death had occurred. It seemed to them a bad omen. And in a sense they were right. Since it was true that at a certain point you might live in a house, and at another point, typically later, you would die. "Hmm, it's not my listing, as you know . . . I think maybe they moved to Montenegro? Or was it Monaco. I can certainly research it for you."

The sheikh had actually lost his temper when the daughter said the house depressed her; he let loose a blistering stream of angry Arabic. But his daughter was spoiled and stubborn. Almost a week of showing them houses, and in the end he'd put her up at a hotel in Beverly Hills, where she would live in a suite. For four years.

Here were the new clients, the dictator, his driver and another guy she hadn't met before. Frankly she could picture any one of them holding a machete. The driver was a white guy from South Africa, she'd guessed last time from the accent, and the new man, black like the dictator, was huge and muscle-bound. They were more like bodyguards than drivers/handlers, actually. Did weapons bulge under their jackets?

"Hello," said the driver. The other two just nodded in greeting.

She smiled, welcomed them in, stood back as they filed past. She'd worn three-inch wedges instead of four-inch pumps, in case, like the sheikh, they were opposed to loose women.

That was the thing about American men; in a way it was comforting. When push came to shove, no woman could be too loose for them.

The dictator stepped through the doorway second; the other two seemed to be bracketing him. Maybe the bodyguard in back, his shoulders broad as a wall, was supposed to take the main guy's head-bullet. She glanced out at their Land Rover, shining on the driveway. Silver and top-of-the-line; it retailed at 200K, if she remembered right from Bobby T.'s boring car monologues in the break room. She had to drive a status car too, in her line of work, so she paid through the nose for the lease, but some joker had rear-ended it yesterday in a parking lot and now the bumper was hanging half-off. It wasn't presentable. She'd had to park it on the street.

For a second she expected to see the glint of a gun in the sun. Barrel protruding from a Japanese maple.

She closed the door.

The three men stood at the picture window with their backs to her, looking out over the canyon, the downtown skyline in the distance. This house always seemed to be waiting for the mudslide that would drag it down the cliff, snagging those giant, spiky plants as it fell. Chunks of frame and plaster would be dangling off plant stalks as beds and espresso makers tumbled down the hillside. Till that day came: 2.8 million, if you don't mind.

She was fine living in the flats. Sure, a fault line might split open into an abyss beneath your feet.

It still seemed like a better bet.

"Let me show you the exterior space," she said, and opened the doors onto the deck. She told them the square footage, mentioned the multicolored underwater lights in the lap pool. Personally she thought the lights were a little Miami, but you never knew what could impress buyers. They followed her down to the pool area, where the driver and bodyguard milled around and the dictator positioned himself at the far end, staring into the water. "Now," she said, "it's not *quite* as striking in daytime, of course, but you can make the water pink or yellow, a whole range of colors, you see?" which she demonstrated by flipping the wall switches.

"What was that movie where the kid got electrocuted?" asked the bodyguard.

She glanced over her shoulder quickly, but the driver and dictator weren't near. The bodyguard had to be addressing her. He was towering but had a handsome face. Almost sweet.

"This little kid dove into a pool at this party, but the lights under the water were broken. The poor kid got electrocuted. Died right away. You know which movie I'm talking about?"

"Sorry, I think I may have missed that one."

"Matt Damon," said the bodyguard, nodding, and walked away from her.

"OK, let's keep going," said the driver. The dictator wasn't coming with them but staying by the pool. He hadn't moved in a while. Gazing at his reflection. Either that or he'd seen something else in the pool that obsessed him. Maybe, staring into the turquoise shallows, he was hallucinating—scenes from his younger days, some old-time genocides. Long-lost machetes danced before his eyes. The leopard-skin hat had no brim; well, sunstroke might drive him inside eventually. She led the other two upstairs, showed them the third and fourth bedrooms and sauna.

She always wondered, when she showed that second-floor bathroom, if anyone other than her would ever notice the book. *The 120 Days of Sodom*. Memorable title. So far no client had mentioned it, but why would they? The cover was drab, no pictures of bodies. See? The driver had walked right past the bathroom door without even glancing in. Not the type for his-and-hers sinks.

Would they like the book if they read it? Parts of it described gleeful murdering.

Her phone rang, unknown number but she didn't like to miss a possible client. No one was going to buy today. Anyway she had nothing to gain from bird-dogging.

"I need to take a quick call," she said to the bodyguard, who had opened a hall closet and appeared to be scrutinizing linens. She walked outside onto a guest balcony adjusting an earbud. From here she had a view of the dictator below. He still stood motionless.

The caller, a certain Sheila, wanted to visit one of her listings mid-Wilshire: a modest home, six figures. Sheila, at least, was a relatable buyer, wisely preferring the earthquake/chasm area over this vertical, parking-challenged, erosion/mudslide/wildfire zone. Showing houses to women was easier because she never thought of attacks. A woman *had* tried to attack her only a couple of weeks ago, actually, whereas a man had never attacked her. Technically. But the female attack had been a freak occurrence, and not too serious either. The attacker was hysterical because of a foreclosure— her emotion was understandable, if not the flurry of weak-fisted blows. In the end, she'd given up easily and slunk away.

Statistically speaking, the next attacker would have to be a man. Maybe several.

Time to go, probably, before the assault got underway.

She saw the driver before he saw her; he was standing in front of a full-length mirror in a guest bedroom looking at himself. He was striking a pose, she could swear, his chest puffed out a bit.

She stepped back, silent as a cat.

South Africans were rumored to be rapists. The white ones especially.

She ran scenarios, that was all. She wasn't clinically paranoid. But someday, would the odds line up against her?

"OK," she called out, "how're we doing in here? Did you have any questions for me?"

And she stepped forward again, into the doorway. The driver had snapped out of his mirror pose and quickly pretended to be looking at a plant.

"I'd be happy to work up a list, if you like," she said. "If you'd just tell me what you're looking for, give me a sense of your wish list . . . you know? I know it's tempting to browse online, but you can't always make these calls based on the MLS photos . . ."

"Yeah, no," he said.

"Why don't you take that to Mr. Diallo. See what he says. OK? Otherwise—"

"Blind leading the blind," said the driver agreeably, turning from the plant and fixing his eyes on her. The pupils seemed very big. As big as dinner plates. Was he stoned?

Were they all stoned?

Now they seemed sluggish in their movements, when she thought back. Not grim, not stern—more slow, like three-toed sloths. Things nested in a sloth. She'd seen it on TV. Sloths' hair was long and greasy. Animal hippies.

"Ryan? Ry! Ry!" someone was yelling. The bodyguard's voice had an urgent tone.

"Lynn?" called the driver—Ry—but he was already running back along the hall, then thumping down the stairs. She followed, not so fast, because the wedge heels were narrow on the bottom. When she came out the back sliders all three were in the pool, fully dressed. At first she didn't recognize the dictator without his hat. They were pulling him out of the water, lifting him up onto the lip. His dripping limbs flopped.

Her own legs went fluid; her arms were hanging.

Then the big man—Lynn—was doing CPR. Odd that he had a girl's name.

"I'm calling 911! I'm calling 911!" she shouted. Her phone was shaking in her hand, trembling so hard she couldn't dial. "Siri. Call 911." *Calling emergency services in five seconds.*

She thought of the front gate—how did you leave it open? She only knew how to *buzz* it open, but then it closed automatically. She had no idea how to *leave* it open—she had to, for the ambulance—should she wait out front? Oh: the operator said they already had the code. Right.

Lynn was on mouth-to-mouth duty while Ryan pumped the chest. She'd always meant to take a course in CPR . . . what if the others hadn't been here? She shivered. She couldn't control it. Now she knew what that meant, *shivering uncontrollably* . . . but they had it covered, didn't they? They'd probably seen their share of death and dying. Bodies that floated down the Zambezi. She thought of "Great Rivers of the World," a page in the family atlas. She'd often stared at it when her mother was locked in her room crying. Bad thought; block it. They didn't have a TV back then. The atlas's filled-in shapes were so satisfying, how they brought space into those smooth, flat pages, both space and fullness, perfect borders and free air . . . the fields of pastels, fine lines like the edge of lace or a leaf. Oceans two-thirds of the planet's body, the blue rivers its veins as they shot through the continents.

Congo, Niger, Zambezi. Across the world, along those veins, bodies floated when war struck the land. Refugees fled from Somalia. They fled from Syria. Afghanistan. Sudan. By the millions. She knew. She read the news.

Next to the flotillas of bodies, a Hollywood lap pool was child's play.

"Not responding," said Ryan, on the brink of tears. "Bloody Christ. God*damn*." Wait. Now he sounded Australian.

Lynn shook his head and muttered, "Keep going, Ry. Just keep going. Don't give up."

She heard the ghost of her own voice, back at the office in the future, telling a story of death by water. Guilt dragged at her—but then Lynn jerked his head back and the dictator was spitting out water and coughing. They turned him on his side and patted him.

Yes! She wanted to leap over the pool and join them—celebrate. But it wasn't her victory. She was a bystander.

They didn't notice her, faded into the background there, but she pushed herself forward unseen. No one could know how much she felt. So glad, so glad!

He was OK.

A cool wind rose from the deep canyon; a siren wound down into silence.

In the book the libertines tortured people. The guy who wrote it had been in prison at the time, locked up in a stone tower. It was revenge porn written by a convict, basically. Mostly just dirty because you felt how desperate the guy was to get off.

For him freedom meant doing exactly what you wanted all the time.

Was that freedom for everybody?

The siren was closer, so she turned and went through the house to get the door.

Two paramedics. Burly, like fireman clichés. With a stretcher.

"Through here. They revived him!" she offered giddily.

Maybe he'd fainted from heat exhaustion and fallen in. Her fault for wishing sunstroke on him—that brought her down, flattened the arc. She would have guessed he could swim, though. Maybe he'd hit his head after fainting. And who knew what might have happened with the owner, with liability—she didn't know how homeowner's insurance worked in a case like this, if she herself might be blamed—a selfish thought, of course. Banish. But practical concerns intruded when you didn't want them to. Reflexes, that was all: a rubber hammer on your knee.

The bodyguards looked up as she trailed the medics to the pool area, stepped back at the medics' approach. They let the other men bend down beside their charge. Ryan watched for a minute, then seemed reassured. He stripped off the jacket he wore, held it by the shoulders and snapped it to dry it off; Lynn was bare to the waist the next time she glanced his way. A tattoo of fine branches laden with white blossoms.

He came over to talk to her—she wished he was wearing a shirt, because of the muscles/embarrassment, but still, it was nice of him to come over.

"Thanks for calling," he said.

"Do you know what—?"

He had a curious look on his face, pinched. Still tense from the near miss. "He suffers from depression."

Something seemed to be swimming in the hot tub—small and orange-brown, it churned in the jets' turbulence.

"His hat," she said, and bent down to fish it out.

Fine orange fibers were coming off on her fingers. Fur wouldn't do that.

"Thanks," said Lynn, and reached out his hand. She laid the hat on it. It was hard not to look at the branches spreading on his broad chest. Her gaze stayed on it a second too long. "A cherry tree," he told her.

"Excuse me?"

"Some cherry trees have white blossoms," he explained. "I didn't want to go with pink."

She wished she could ask him about the depression. Was there a nice word for *dictator*? But she didn't believe that anymore. A dictator who wore fake fur? She doubted it. Who'd told her he was an African despot to begin with? Michelle the B of A lender? Michelle had said he had no credit so they couldn't prequalify, but it turned out he didn't need a mortgage. Someone ran a verification of funds and it was moot: Mr. Diallo was cash-rich.

"I like it," she said. And it was true—she liked the flowers and she liked the branches. Their delicacy.

"He has these bouts," said Lynn. "You name it. Between you and me, since you've seen—well, depression, agoraphobia, social anxiety . . . it's worse when we're recording. More pressure. The label's—you know. Excuse my language, but—assholes."

Creatives.

"Oh," she said. "You're *musicians*."

"Well, he is, anyway. Ry plays the bass. I'm just a drummer," he said, and smiled.

Ryan was stoned for certain. At least she'd called that one.

The medics had the musician on their gurney; she glanced quickly at him as they pushed past, wheels squeaking.

"Should be OK, but we do need to take him in," a medic said.

"I'm fine," whispered the musician, though she could barely hear him.

"Sure. We'll follow you," said Ryan.

Lynn was wringing out his wet shirt, wincing in distaste as he pulled it on again.

Social anxiety, not religion. She could have worn the pumps. One of the medics stopped the gurney a couple of feet away and talked into his headset. Meanwhile the musician lay helpless beneath her gaze, lit by the sun. He was exposed; she could look at him now, since his eyes were closed.

He seemed so young. She hadn't known how young he was.

Those hands had never touched a machete.

Lynn was beside her, waiting for the medics to get moving again.

"You can call me," she told him.

"Of course," he said. "He'll still want—he really needs to find a place."

That wasn't what she meant.

"Call me for *any* reason," she said. Had she said it? When you were this relieved it was like being drunk. It let you melt into the air—but not only the air.

It was hard to let yourself drown, they said; a will to live kicked in. Maybe he had been asking himself, as he stood there at the end of the lap pool, if he could do it. In a way he'd proved he could. Because he hadn't saved himself, he hadn't jumped into the pool, sunk down, and then surfaced again spluttering. He'd stayed the course and let the water in. The water had entered his lungs. Someone else had saved him.

So maybe his question had been answered. Can I? Yes.

She walked them to the driveway, watched as the paramedics loaded him into the ambulance and Lynn and Ryan climbed into their car. From the driver's seat, Lynn slid down his window. It made a purring sound.

"So I'll call you," he said. "Nina. Right?"

"Yes. Call. I hope you do," and she stepped a bit closer. Beyond

him in the shadows of the interior Ryan was wiping his sunglasses. "And—tell me how he's doing."

"Sure thing," said Lynn.

She watched them back out, watched the gate close on its slow
rollers. She had to do the rounds, lock up before she left.

She went from room to room, checking the staging was still
right. She'd had clients who moved things around, who ate the
food out of strangers' refrigerators. One guy had eaten a whole
pint of ice cream while she was showing his wife a property's
backyard. Just took it out of the sellers' freezer, sat down at the
kitchen island and spooned it all up. When she and the wife came
back in he was chucking the empty container into the sink.

Not the garbage. The sink.

He didn't even hide the evidence. A libertine, clearly.

What could she do with herself? Shaken, then so relieved . . .
what happened next? The rest of the day felt spare, like: what was
it for? Busy. And also empty.

In the bathroom she glanced at the book but didn't touch
it. The first line she'd ever seen in the book came back to her:
"There's more to it than simply having a comely ass, you know."

Maybe, after she showed the place on Orange Street to Sheila,
she'd drive back up here early for the 3:30 and hope for a page
that told about the turning of the virgins . . . most of the pages
disgusted her, true, and parts were laughable, but along the edges
there was sex. The virgins had to be pried open—was she a pervert,
or just bored? Maybe there *were* no perverts anymore. There was
a huge industry: perverts were business, that was all. Like everything. She'd looked up the book. It had been written during the
French Revolution, when the Marquis de Sade was in prison, and
a few years after he got out he was arrested again, this time by

Napoleon. His last girlfriend—from when he was seventy years old until he died in an asylum at seventy-four—was fourteen.

The book had been banned in various countries, according to Siri/Wikipedia, for *extreme violence and pornography*. But now it was bathroom décor.

Look around. The libertines had won.

She felt the euphoria drain away. What stayed was almost like grief. It was true someone had been saved, but who was saved and who was left?

How many were left sinking under, with no one watching them?

Her mother, for instance. The water had been pills, but all the same. No one.

Into the air went their panic, unheard. Into the air went agony. The sky must be full of it.

She flicked the lights out as she stepped through the sliders to the back deck. You couldn't leave the jets on in the hot tub.

The pool water's surface was still, and around it the tiles were bone-dry. The homeowners wouldn't know what happened here, just her and the guys and the medics—it hadn't happened for them. To them the pool when they got home from work would be identical to the pool they left this morning.

Well, she would have to disclose, of course. The 911 call. Of course. Would they be billed for it? She'd look that up, too. But without her disclosure they would see the same pool. A pool without this history.

A man like Lynn was a form of protection, a human fortress. *There is an enemy at the gates.*

As she got older she was drawn to men with heft; you didn't want a slight man as the years wore on. You knew the world better

now than when you were young, you knew your own weakness.
A fortress could help.

Was there an enemy at the gates?

Anyway this man *did* protect—not even afraid of mouth-to-
mouth. Not squeamish. No one had given him permission; no
one had conferred authority on him. He'd stepped up, accepted
his role without a qualm. If he did call her, she would speak out
and say she admired him. He was a good man. Were there fewer
of them now, good men and good women? Solid and capable? Or
was it just the lifestyle that made it seem that way?

Too often the future was somewhere else, a land where you
might find yourself one day. There was no need to travel there on
purpose. Easy to tell yourself the future could be staved off and
nothing had to change: the present would stretch in a band of
gold along the horizon, bright line joining the earth and sky.

As she went out she caught sight of the fountain in the front,
where she'd never seen water: it was dry. A small cement fountain
with a statue on it, a cherub holding a bunch of grapes. Cradling
them in his hands. Why was unclear. A cherub with grapes, a
figure she didn't understand.

Fear could turn you into a statue. Some people were statues all
their lives. They feared the freedom of others, that others' freedom could end up hurting them. A person might want to be free
to do something to you, often. One man's freedom was another
man's aggravated assault.

But then, if you stood still like that, you couldn't go anywhere.
And was it fair to blame the libertines for moving?

The libertines dined at a long table, drank until they were drunk.
They spun and danced and deflowered virgins, while all around
them, stricken, stood statues in poses of humility and confusion.

BREAKFAST AT TIFFANY'S

His mother had told him he had to get out for the so-called "showing," which was during school hours anyway, but no. If they wanted to see his room, they could see it with him inside. And if it made some rich guy not want to buy the house, so good. So, QED. A Latin saying you used in math proofs, if you were fool enough to do them. *Quod erat demonstrandum.* "Which had to be proven."

He didn't want to leave, hell no. The other option was some crap condo, some downsized piece of shit. He saw it already, he didn't have to see it to see it. Beige carpets. Paper-thin walls and hollow doors. Maybe one of those pools in the middle, dirty, with a couple spindly palm trees leaning over and rotting leaves floating. Concrete steps up to the second-floor catwalk. No thanks, *mater*.

She wouldn't know till after. She was at work, while he was cutting school. An often-preferred activity. Preferred activities: watching, listening, gaming. Not school-working. Other preferred activities: getting off, three to five times per day. Minimum. Smoking, say five to ten. Also, nothing. Nothing was a preferred activity for damn certain.

What he had planned for this afternoon's showing was nothing short of diabolical: perform preferred activities in his bedroom. If the potential house-buyers came in, so much the better and let them feast their eyes on him. *In flagrante delicto*. First righteous saying Mr. Devon had ever taught them, which got him into the Romans. "In the very act of wrongdoing."

So here he was, ensconced. He had the pillows set up in imperial fashion and he lounged back against them, remote like a royal scepter. Jeans off and boxer briefs tugged down. Before him, the viewing altar. Flat-screen, HD, like everyone's, but even larger than you often saw. Big-ass. He'd made them get him a big-ass TV back when they had money. For his viewing pleasure. Now here it was.

For accompaniment he'd chosen old music. Liked vintage. His tastes were rarefied, admittedly. This in particular: Sid Vicious, of the old school of punk rockers. Helped his lady OD, then OD'd himself. There was a movie about it. But this was another scene. This was some video by French people. Some Eurofags who digged the Vish, back in the day. Who wouldn't? Even the French dug him. Even back then.

Before a stage curtain came Sid, and grabbed a mic on a tall stand. He sang the song, a cover of a Blue-Eyes tune. That Frank

Sinatra. Also dead. Gangsta himself, they said, back then, though more of a mafioso type. And here came Vicious to cover him. He'd changed the words. He sang his own version. It was supposed to be some cheesy crooner thing, but he sang other words. "My Way." Hard to understand at first, because the Vish yelled more than sang.

And at the end of the vid, he pulled out a machine gun and sprayed the audience with gunfire. The Eurofags toppled in their seats.

When it was over, briefly a silence fell. From downstairs he could hear voices. Good: the house gawkers were here. He'd play the Vish again later, but now for porn. She'd taken the lock off his bedroom door—said she didn't *want* to do it, of course, but he'd "abused his right to privacy." He put it on again, knew how to use a cordless drill, but off it came again as soon as she discovered it.

So now she'd reap what she sowed. *In flagrante*, mamacita. Lubriderm in the drawer. Kleenex. This one was a blond chick in Carpinteria. About his age, he figured, *ergo*, under—. She did a bunch of different stuff, but his preferred modalities were, in descending order, (1) Coy Cheerleader, (2) Daddy's Good Good Little Girl, and (3) Catwoman.

Sometimes, though the black-latex suit ruled, he got bored of Catwoman. Too much hissing and meowing. The scratching moves could last for ages, to where he wanted to say, Chick, listen, you are *way* too into this. She had these long metal claws that, come to think of it, looked more like Wolverine's, and liked to raise her hands one at a time and curl the claws down and pretend to be mauling him. The viewer. Whoever. It wasn't that cute. More annoying.

He brought her up, click-click.

"I'm ready whenever you are, big boy," she said.

She wasn't dumb, though. A few times they'd messaged. Her clichés were ironic.

The cheer itself was nothing to write home about, although he liked the pink pom-poms. It was pure warm-up. The bouncing parts, *mammilla* and *glutei*, got you ready. Plus the trick that ended when she stood with her legs apart, bent over, and looked at him through the upside-down V. Her music sucked major wad, some stupid teeny-bopper shit she listened to ironically, but still stupid.

And worse, not loud enough.

Knock-knock.

"Someone in there?" called out a woman from beyond the door.

He wouldn't dignify it with a response. The door was closed; if she should choose to violate, that was on her. On her own head be it.

The stripper-cheerleader took off her bra and squeezed them together, round balloons. Two pink eyes, ogling him. Faster.

"Yoo-hoo," said the woman's voice. "You know, this is the teenager's room. He might have left the music on when he went out to school."

Faster, faster—and then it happened. *Flagrante.* Quick blur of a face: the woman he'd met before, the house-selling agent.

"Oh my—!" The door slammed shut in a hurry.

Yes! New record. She had a hot mouth, the agent. Great when it hung open like that, in a perfect blowup-doll O. She wasn't bad overall, for someone in the aged set.

The cheerleader kept on going. It wasn't a two-way video feed. *He* did the watching. Not the help.

Murmurs outside the door. He felt a grin spreading. Reached for the Kleenex. There you go. *Veni, vidi, vici.* Julius Caesar *shit.*

Then silence again. The home invaders had moved on. Continuing their tour. Bully for them. He hoped she *did* tell Mrs. Mom. He hoped she did. Would show she had a pair on her. Plus it'd be interesting, what happened next. It'd be a science experiment to witness his mother's embarrassment. Surely she'd try to "have a talk" with him. Of course, she knew his habits; they were no secret. *Shee-yit,* the laundry didn't wash itself. In the OT, Jahweh killed Onan for spilling his seed on barren ground. Harsh.

His mother didn't go Jahweh on him—the opposite. She'd said more than once that it was *developmentally appropriate.* Although lately she'd suggested, better in moderation. "Maybe . . . also focus on other interests?"

Still: a public shaming was different. Him acting out. Giving offense. Well, let her struggle. As mortals did. His role was that of anthropologist. Observe the tribe of others. His mission. The world was made of primitives.

But his guess was, the agent lady wouldn't breathe a word. Not real enough. None of them were. They said nothing. They talked and talked, but you could swap out their words for other words, like at random, and nobody would notice the difference.

"I'm good," he told Carpinteria. "Check you later."

"Whoa, that was quick."

"I had some help," he said, and cut the connection. She had his card on file. Well, mamacita's card. Technically.

Time for some face. A face-to-face encounter. He switched back to the vid of Sid. Ratcheted the volume right up to 11. Another vintage ref.

Pulled on his pants, went out the door. Left wadded Kleenex and Lubriderm on bed. Stagecraft.

Down the hallway, he found the group of them in the master suite. Here was where his mother slept, all by her lonely now that the Dadster was deadbeat. Big bed. A California king. The gawkers stood looking into the bathroom. Like a toilet could full-on fascinate. The greatest show on Earth! A sink! And a toilet!

Losers.

Plenty of them—six, he counted. All over the hill. A bunch of human sacks, floppy, including a guy with a beer belly.

They turned.

"Oh, um," said the house-selling woman. "Ah. Jeremy. Hi there."

Ron Jeremy to you, lady.

"Hey ho," he said. "How's it hangin'. You can show them my room now, if you like."

"Oh, that's all right," she said. "We wouldn't want to, uh, disturb—"

"No, really. It's a great room," he said, wearing a smile. She wasn't going to get off that easy. "Got my own balcony. It's on the other side from this. View of the Capitol Records building. Home of the Beastie Boys. *Super.*"

That last he said real kiss-ass style. He'd never say "super" normally.

"Sure," said the beer belly heartily. "Sure! Come on, folks! Let's go take a look!"

So they trooped after him, back down the hall. He didn't look behind him, but you could bet the house-selling woman was lagging. She was the only one who'd gotten a real gander.

He threw open the door to chaos land. His walls had several

posters on them, including some purchased mail-order from the *Hustler* store.

On the big screen Vish was still yelling.

"You cunt, I'm not a queer / I'll state my case, of which I'm certain."

Sid was right on the sorry homophobe brief. Right on it. Some old-school homophobe shit. It dated him, but fuck. He was still Sid.

"Nice décor, son," said the fat man, while the older ladies adjusted their expressions. Onscreen, Sid wielded his weapon, and bullets sprayed the French people. Totally fake-looking of course. You couldn't believe it for even a second.

Back then they had no CGI. All their FX were retarded.

"Thanks, man," he said, whilst taking in the ladies, whose eyes alighted in passing on the tissue and lubricant. Then darted off again.

"The view of *outside*, anyway," said the house woman, crossing the patches of floor between the heaps of soiled laundry like they were stepping stones through hot lava, "is impressive," and she pulled open the curtains. Light flooded in.

The ladies were reluctant to cross the lava flow. Beer-belly man not so; he crushed the clothes beneath his giant feet.

"Can we go out?" he asked, and the saleswoman opened the slider. "Oh yeah," he called, from beyond. "Nice. Great panorama. As good as the master."

But the ladies were in a rush to leave. In no time only he, the man, and the house-selling woman remained. The two of them stood on his balcony, jawing too quiet to hear, and when they came back in the man stood in front of him, confronting-like. Reached out and took him by the shoulders. Actual skin contact.

"Tough times," he said. "I was a pissant too, at your age. It passes."

Answer not ready. Answer not formerly prepared, dammit.

Fall back on Latin. The Romans had something for him. He searched his lexicon.

"*Caveat emptor*, dude," he said.

"Let the buyer beware?"

He nodded at the man sagely, though truth be told, hadn't expected the guy to translate it.

"You like Latin?"

Oh no. He wasn't falling into that trap. No heart-to-heart with beer belly for the fatherless kid.

"Hate it," he said.

"I get it," said the guy. "It's all about the hating."

"Well, Jeremy, we'll leave you to your private activities," said the woman, and walked past him and out the door. She smelled of something good. Warm, not too sweet, not chemical at all, but with a touch of spice to it. Familiar.

The man grinned, shook his head.

"You'll be OK," he said. "But. You think we're all assholes. You won't hear this. I'll still say it. Hating's easy. Couldn't be easier. It's just a default setting. The easy way out. It's all the rest that's actually hard."

Then he turned and galumphed through the door.

Shit save him from turning into a guy like that.

But he didn't feel like watching now. He let the screen go blank. He didn't want content. Content be damned. He wanted to be empty, empty like a glass. Transparent.

Out in the hall again, he listened for a while. After a time he heard the front door close. Weird; he was almost disappointed. Bad to have people here, but somehow worse in the aftermath.

He wandered back toward the mamacita's lair. On her vanity there were cosmetics by the score. Once he'd seen a price tag on a pot of her face cream: four hundred bucks. That was so desperate. The lotions and the powders hadn't helped.

When he was little, sometimes they'd gone to parties without him. Beforehand she'd let him watch her dress. Nothing too perv, she always had a lacy slip on by the time she let him in. He used to watch her put up her hair. Like in the movies: rich kids watched their mothers get ready. Good feeling. Dinner parties and evening wear. She'd been so deft with bobby pins it looked like sleight of hand. Magic, he called it then. He flashed to one time when her long hair, in the space of a few seconds, was transformed into a great shining round atop her head.

That shit looked *elegant*. Audrey Hepburn. "Magic, mama." She picked him up and twirled him. He'd been so small. Hard to believe.

He held one lipstick, then another. He sat down in her chair. If he were more cross-dressing, he'd cover his face in all her makeup shit. But that wasn't his bag. Though true, it would be perfect maternal horror-show. He'd freak her out, when she came home, if he was done up all clownish and faux-femme. That'd be a fast ride to prescribed counseling, although his mother would also say—like she had said about that neighbor kid—*gender fluidity is perfectly natural*. Still, counseling would be called for, which he, of course, would never attend. "You don't *want* to hurt me, Jemmy. I *know* you don't. You know how much I love you. You're all I'm living for."

There were also perfumes, bottles dusty. The deadbeat used to give her those. He picked up a bottle, spritzed here and there. You could watch the vapor descend. If he were more stoned, he'd spritz them till they were all empty. She'd never know. Didn't use them. Just kept the bottles there, like rows of soldiers keeping watch. Shit yeah. Slight clouds. They settled on the vanity's counter, dulling the brown shine, darkening the denim over his knees.

That was the smell. One of the perfumes was the same the house-selling woman wore. It made him remember . . . or no, it made him *want* to remember. He couldn't reach it. Back when he wasn't old enough to know himself—that was when it was from.

Velut arbor ita ramus. "Just like the tree, so is the branch." Never never. She showed her sadness like a split bone poking out of her skin. Compound fracture. A form of nakedness that could never be attractive.

Well, not him.

"I show no bones," he said aloud.

The guy with the beer belly had it wrong. Not hatred, just anger. There was a difference. One was like rock, the other like fire. The ancient elements.

Sure, fire burned. It was supposed to. It scorched and made stuff black, everything brown or black or ash-gray. Burn and scorch, throw flames, spray paint. Tag *everything*, holmes. He owed no apologies. And anyway, that tint was real. The world was covered in it.

The world, when you looked at it coldly, was tinted with anger. The screech of rubber on asphalt. Metal and concrete.

He was letting that beer-belly Santa give him a lump of coal. This down feeling. Forget it—no. Had Santa brought it, though? Or had the coal been sitting there? The coal *had* been sitting there. Since *paterfamilias* had left, sowing his seed in younger soil.

The Dadster's clichés weren't ironic. He really meant that shit.

Himself, he'd stopped believing in Santa by first grade. The big kids down the street gave him the 411. All harsh, like *Fucking*

Santa? You must be a moron. Too bad. When you believed, the world was tinted differently . . . like "Magic, mama," and then she lifted you. Because you were small, you could be held, flown through the air and delighted, like that single moment was the same as forever.

Back then, you didn't even worry about feelings. You hadn't learned to pity yet. You didn't need anger if you didn't feel pity.

He had to do something. *Doing* never, lately, among preferred activities. And yet, if the shoe fit . . . but what could he even do?

She liked flowers. *Adored* flowers, she once said. Simple. Easy. Not asking so much. Was it? But she never got them. Not anymore.

She was a baby bird on the sidewalk, flapping with broken wings. When he thought about her he was close to feeling that brittle snap himself. His own wrist. Or a leg cracking. It wouldn't be the pain he minded but the helplessness.

*Bull*shit.

He had her card.

That shit, now he could *do*. Not one bunch, not even ten. A house of flowers. True, they were strapped for cash. *Ergo*, selling. But if—she said they were in bankruptcy. She said they were headed for Chapter Eleven. Like volume at 11, just like that vintage *Spinal Tap* hilarity. Turn the volume up to 11. He'd Googled they forgave all debts. In Chapter Eleven.

Part of the reason he didn't feel so bad about the Coy Cheerleader. It was just digits into the morass. Drop in the ocean. OK, so, several drops.

That was the plan. Nothing fancy. Plain and simple. House full of flowers. Not cut flowers because they died too fast. They'd die all at once, turn the house into a brown forest of death. Too depressing. No, flowers in pots—that plant place she liked on Sunset. Silverlake. He'd bring them back in truckloads. What did he have—three hours? Or four if she worked late. Maybe he'd have them delivered. Money was no object.

When she walked in, a thousand blooms. No gray or brown there. Orange, yellow and red. *Transit umbra, lux permanet.* "The shadow passes, but the light remains."

A part of her, sure, would be quite amply pissed. The rest of her would remember, even when he was gone. Moved out, too old to live at home. For all the time after, when she would have to be alone.

He went down to the garage, took the keys off the hook and got into the work truck. The only solid thing Lord Vader had left them. Waited as the garage door cranked up, waited longer as a nanny passed on the sidewalk with a stroller in front of her and a little kid toddling behind. The rich parents were the only even half-smart ones: outsourcing. He'd never gotten what was in it for parents. You saw them everywhere, fussing around their kids, doing dumb small shit. Always bent over fastening things, unfastening them, wiping the offspring, pushing or pulling them, sitting them in small chairs, rolling them, swinging them, feeding them with small spoons. Servants for no money. There was a word for that.

Weird how everyone wanted to act wild, then in the next breath tame. It happened overnight. You partied, then you got married and turned in your balls. You *lined* up to turn them in. Eagerly packaged them, tying a bow on top.

If you didn't have kids there was still a chance, maybe. Because even married, as long as you didn't have kids you could keep doing drugs. Go out a lot.

Nursery, it said on the sign, like the little plants had their own rattles and cribs.

But inside it was disappointing. There weren't as many flowers as he'd expected. There were mostly leaves and stems. Green parts. Even the flowers were mostly lame. Not like starbursts, not like glamour. They just sat there.

God*damn*. Nothing was ever fucking splendid. *Never splendid.* God*damn*.

Was he supposed to go home with a bunch of ass-bushes? Pots of ass-dirt?

Bullshit.

He kicked a pot. Hurt his toe. Looked closer. The blooms on it were seedy and bluish. *Agapanthus. Stevie's Wonder. Sun to Part Sun; Hybrid.*

Seriously? A plant named for Stevie Wonder?

Sick.

"Jeremy?"

No way. Nuh-uh. The new wife. Lora. Pregnant as shit.

"Uh," he said. Grunting ape-like.

"Jeremy! Hey! It's so great to see you! You still haven't been by the *house*! But what are you doing at a *garden* store?"

She reached out and hugged him, her bag sliding off her shoulder and hitting him as the baby bump nudged where it should never go. The floor slanted down, plus she was just the wrong amount shorter than him.

So wrong: through a veil of skin and blubber, his fetal half-sister was barely three inches from his D.

He looked past the new wife's shoulder at a fat frog. It was a planter thing, made out of china or whatever, and out of it stuck a bunch of those ugly flowers you saw on cement doorsteps. Wrinkled. A pylon-color orange. The frog's bulgy, heavy-lidded eyes made it look sly and evil, like it would slurp out a tongue and gulp your head.

"Nothing," he said, pulling back. "Dad here?"

"At work. I wanted to surprise him with some new plantings. I'm not actually putting them in. I can't even touch my toes! Just buying them for the gardener. How about you? You running an errand?"

It was wrecked anyway. Dumb idea.

He shook his head. "I should go."

"Hey. Will you do me a favor first?" she asked, and winced like asking hurt a bit. "Can you come with me? Pull that cart and maybe load my plants into the car? Five minutes, that's it. I promise."

He'd come for the sake of his mother, now here he was serving Public Enemy Number One. Normally he didn't say much to the new wife. Safer that way. She acted nicey-nice, plus she actually seemed to mean it, so it was hard to hate her guts once she got all up in your grill. *Ergo*, he kept his trap shut.

Vir sapit qui pauca loquitur: "He is wise who talks little."

But now she'd cornered him.

He grabbed the handle of the plant wagon, walking behind her to the parking lot. It reminded him of the old Radio Flyer he used to pull around his stuffed animals in. His favorite was a camel that smelled bad from having its foot sucked. Where had the camel gone?

Of course you got too old for toys and didn't use them anymore, all that was fine. But where was the camel?

In a landfill somewhere.

He loaded the plants for her. They were boring.

In the background the child bride chattered on about him

coming to dinner. How the Dadster would be "over the moon" to see him. Total bullshit. His father hadn't been "over the moon" in his life. Over a slut's ass cheeks, maybe. His eyes were dead like a shark's.

Flowers filling the house. What a cheesy idea *that* had been.

Before it had seemed kickass. Now, cheesy and stupid. Clearly a Mary Jane moment.

Slamming down the SUV hatch, he saw a blur of movement along some bushes near his feet. A cat. Small. Gray, with patchy fur. Looked homeless. Did it smell homeless? Could a cat get B.O.?

"Oh my God. Is that a kitten?"

She went scrabbling after it, but she couldn't bend over far enough. Chick was basically a human water balloon, dangling and wobbling on a stick. Stand back! That thing could burst.

She made a wheezing noise, then staggered sideways against her car door.

He'd ask if she was OK, but it wasn't in the bylaws. Whenever it randomly occurred to him to act normal/human to her, he thought of the Dadster hitting that. Made him wish he had the talent of spontaneous puking.

Slowly she righted herself, mouth-breathing.

"That poor little guy's gonna get run over," she said. "Don't you think? All that traffic? Like twenty feet from here? Oh my God. It's just a kitten!"

It was small, sure, but looked ancient. A cat Gandalf. Merlin. A wrinkled graybeard. If it was human, it'd be bent over and carrying some kind of gnarled staff. Gumming and mumbling.

Luckily it wasn't. Say what you like about a decrepit cat, it was still better than a decrepit human.

It faced away from them, tail waving, head under a bush, and then turned around with something in its mouth.

"Oh!" said Lora. "Oh no! Is that a little mouse?"

Child bride thought fleabag feral cats were cute kittens. She thought moldy hotdogs were itty-bitty mice.

She thought his father was a great guy.

He could see the package, greasy litter under the hedge.

"It's, like, a Hebrew National," he said.

She looked relieved. "Hey. But won't you come over later? Please? Just come have dinner with us? It'd be so great!"

He shrugged. She kept staring at him and smiling. All hopeful, like she was hanging on his answer.

Finally he did a half-nod. Grudging. That way, if she tried to hold him to it, he had a way out. What did they call it in the CIA? Deniability. Yeah. Plausible deniability.

On the way home he saw a billboard with a puppy on it. Maybe that was what he should have gotten, a puppy. His mother was allergic to cats but not to dogs. His father never let her have a dog when they were married but she was always drawn to other people's. Scratched them behind the ears, obsessively bought gourmet treats for them. Once she'd driven a platter of leftovers to the pound to give to the homeless pitbulls, waiting to be put to sleep. But the pounds didn't want it. Something about too much cream. So she threw out the platter, right there at the pound.

After, she said to him: "I mean, *this* is exactly what's wrong with the world."

Maybe what she needed wasn't anything like flowers. Maybe that was like, a Band-Aid. Some people let their babies cry for hours, just to teach them to shut the fuck up. Probably worked. But then the babies grew up and turned into psychos.

Still, maybe what she needed *was* tough love. It was too late for her to turn psycho, anyway. Late-onset psycho wasn't a thing. Her shrink didn't do shit, was what it sounded like to him whenever she told him the stuff the shrink had said. Her shrink just basically agreed with her.

He drove the truck into the garage again. Her car was there—she was home.

In the kitchen she stood by the sink. She had cooking stuff out, a pan and some noodles, but she wasn't cooking yet. The water was running and running, just flowing right down the drain, but all she did was stand staring out the window, her hand frozen on the tap. You'd think something amazing was happening outside. A naked marathon.

"I'm going over there," he said abruptly.

He opened the fridge, peered around for sodas. She always said they were bad for his skin. But he'd stashed a couple of cans.

"Going . . . ?" she asked. Her little-girl voice. Distant.

"To his house. For dinner."

The tap was still running and she didn't turn around. He caught a glimpse of the telltale red-and-white logo, pushed aside a lead burrito in tinfoil. Closed the fridge door. Popped the tab.

The Dadster was an asshole, fully certified. But life went on. Actually, it could be funny to watch his dickhead personality play out. Like, comedy. If you put yourself outside it like you were watching a movie, then shit, it could really crack you up.

Step outside, holmes. Then laugh like a hyena.

Plus, the child bride tried to be nice to him 24/7. That baby mama worked *hard*. She had fresh skin, a peaches-and-cream complexion. Even fat with the fetal intruder, she was a yummy mummy. No one could deny it.

He could step outside himself and laugh, but his mother could never. She didn't know how. He went up behind her, reached out with his left hand and turned the water off.

She was still staring out the window. Any second she'd start crying. He knew the signs.

"I went out to get you flowers," he said. It made him nervous to say it now, it was so hokey. But he forced himself. "But none of them were good enough so I didn't get any. Sorry. Anyway then that Lora girl showed up and made me carry plants into her car and nagged at me for like ten straight minutes to come to their house tonight. I had to say yes. She basically tricked me."

It was a lie, but a white lie. Still: enough tough love for now. Just going over there was bad enough.

"It's good, honey," she whispered, nodding. "No, you should go. It's healthy."

But he was supposed to be angry, wasn't he? He did the angry, she did the sad. Division of labor.

"It's good for you to spend time with your father," she said. Turning away, she lifted the back of a hand to her face, maybe wiping a tear, maybe not. Couldn't see.

"I will. But I don't *want* to," he said.

That at least he could give her. Wasn't a house full of flowers. But better than nothing.

"You're sweet. But you don't have to hate him to be loyal to me. Go. Have a nice meal. And if you have to get stoned, wait till you get home."

"I will," he promised. The Dadster typically smelled it on his breath and went Republican, droned on about how stoners would never bring home the big bucks, did he always plan to be an underachiever, how many spare brain cells did he have to waste by killing them. He would a hundred percent wait.

He thought the words *a solemn dignity*. Like a bolt from the blue. Inspiration.

He would be dignified from now on. His earlier, midday self, first jacking off, then flaunting it, was hereby dismissed. That was the old him. This was the new. *A solemn dignity*.

A second cousin of his with Down syndrome had gotten baptized as an adult, if you could call her that when her mind was eight years old till death. Point was she'd wanted to be a Catholic, though her whole family was regular WASPs, because she liked the saints, the stained-glass windows and, as his mother said, "gruesome depictions of the Crucifixion." So she worked hard to learn the lines or whatever, and the parents sent out fancy invitations with gold letters stamped on them, and he had to go. His mother made him wear a suit.

At the time he'd been pissed before they went, because if the cousin hadn't had Down syndrome, he could have stayed at home. Nobody would have given a crap. Baptism? Teenage whim, they would have said. You could bet on it.

But she did have Down syndrome, so on went the tie that felt like it was choking him and the gay shoes that pinched.

In the church she was dressed in a snow-white robe and smiled without end. She beamed. His whole life, he could swear, he'd never seen anyone look that happy.

Do you renounce Satan, the author and prince of sin?

I do.

"I renounce him," he muttered under his breath, exiting the kitchen with the soda can in his grip.

"What, sweetie?"

"Nothing."

And all his works?

I do.

BIRD-HEAD MONSTER

The people who owned the house had an art collection. Actually it was just a bachelor, the real-estate lady said, not even a couple. The place was big. He owned a lot of modern paintings, which to her looked like some kid had brought them home from pre-K. He also had forgeries of Old Masters. The real-estate lady showed her a whole room devoted to the fakes, done by a famous forger. Some looked pretty good, like portraits of queens or stuff. "But Flemish is his specialty," the lady told her as they walked past. She had no idea what Flemish meant. Was it a country or an art style? "Belgian," the lady said.

Like the fluffy waffles. A carb nightmare.

Most buyers didn't look at the art much, because it wasn't

included, the lady went on. But touring this house was like a visit to an art museum. "And free of charge!" she added, smiling.

Not much of a bargain if you didn't *like* the crap. Rand sometimes bought blue-chip stuff, when the art advisor said he should, but this—who knew if it was even bankable. He wanted her to get a sense of whether the place's floors and ceilings were level, whether its lines were flush and clean or old and rough and handmade-looking. You couldn't see those things online. Check out the sunken baths, he said. Am I going to have to rip them out *right* away? Can I even have guests over with that shit? Or can I wait? Because the renovation budget, for this tax year, shouldn't go above a million.

"Mint," said the real-estate agent in the kitchen. "All-new appliances. He wasn't planning to move. The fridge is a Sub-Zero . . ."

"Rand's over the whole brushed-stainless deal," she told her, shrugging. "He wants slate. We'd have to replace it all. And he hates white-marble countertops. He says they're too nineties."

"I see," said the lady, cocking her head. "Hmm. Well, I could see that if it were granite, but this is a really fine Italian—"

"He likes this place mostly for the location." It was six minutes from here to his brand-new office. And that was at rush hour.

"If you did go the kitchen remodel route, you could resell. This range? It hasn't even been used and it retails near a hundred thousand."

"Mmm," she said. As if they'd go around hawking secondhand appliances. Should she be insulted? She didn't look like someone who should be insulted. Everything she wore was couture. Surely she couldn't be mistaken for a hawker of used goods. She felt a spark of contempt for the woman—probably didn't know real Dolce from Chinese knockoffs. Although, maybe she was just doing her job. Due diligence. That was a thing. They'd already been through four real-estate agents, none of them up to Rand's standards. This one, at least, seemed to have a basic grasp. Though possibly Rand had picked her for her tits. Perky and round at the same time. They couldn't be real.

But she was way too sensitive, she knew. Rand said it too—she had delicate sensibilities. A sign of refinement, but also, she had to work on hiding it. It's a dog-eat-dog world, Rand liked to remind her. "I'm not a dog," she always said. Then Rand pretended to pet her, asked if she'd beg him for a treat. Ruff-ruff. She smiled. Their little secret.

The lady was leading her out of the kitchen. They passed again through the fake-paintings room, big and almost empty. Just a sofa against a wall, that was it. And paintings everywhere. A big painting caught her eye, lots of different colors. Three panels hinged together. Little animals and weird creatures all over it.

"They say that's the finest Bosch forgery in the world," said the woman. "The side panels represent heaven and hell."

The right side was hideous. *So* ugly. She bent in, looking closer. A monster sat in a highchair, eating a person whose butt and legs stuck out of his ugly beak. The person's ass was naked, and out of it flew black birds. The monster had a bird's head too.

"Dis*gust*ing!" she exclaimed.

"Well," said the woman, "I guess that's hell for you."

She never understood why painters made ugly things. A, who wanted them in their house? This guy, obviously . . . who had no taste, or anyway was stuck in the nineties. And 2, it seemed like showing off. Like, hey, this is ugly! In your *face*.

People were rude and called it art.

Well, the place was big enough. Rand liked the square footage.

A good footprint to work with, he had said. She was ready to call him in. She screened the properties for him; the ones that made it past her were only the serious contenders.

"I'm going to call Rand," she told the real-estate lady. "OK? I think he'll come, if I tell him to."

"Sure," said the lady, after a moment's hesitation. "I do have another appointment, but I can push it back."

He said he'd be there in half an hour. She'd have to do the tour again with him, so meantime she'd play Jelly Jump. It got the adrenaline flowing. She walked onto the terrace, found a lounge chair. Her top score was 56; she'd beat it today, she resolved. Time flew when she was playing Jelly Jump, though once the real-estate agent came out and interrupted her. She didn't stop playing but her concentration was ruined and her jelly drowned in black goo. She tried not to snap. *No,* she didn't want a glass of ice water. What if the lady brought her tap? No thanks. *Jesus.*

Because of that interruption, probably, she was only at 49 when he arrived, way later than he'd said.

Rand wasn't punctual, but she'd gotten used to it.

He was doing a call on his headset and didn't greet the real-estate woman when she opened the door for him, just flapped a hand to show she shouldn't talk and nodded to show they should start walking. The three of them toured the house in silence except for his half of the call. He was in commodities, the words he said an unbreakable code.

But it felt a little weird, going through rooms without the real-estate agent saying anything. Once or twice he would lean in to look at something, shoot the agent a question she didn't have the answer to but said she would research. Rand didn't acknowledge her when she said that; it probably confirmed his opinion that she, like almost everyone, was not as smart as him. People were always confirming his opinions.

Although she did catch him resting his eyes on the real-estate woman's ass. *Bottom*. Well, anyone would. The skirt was too tight, frankly. And off the rack, but that went without saying . . . He kept the woman walking ahead of him, she noticed. He obviously liked the view. But the woman was older than she was, probably had over a decade on her. Though still younger than Rand. But not younger enough. Right? And not *as* pretty, not by far. Anyone would agree. She had crow's-feet, and lines on her forehead when she made an expression. No Botox, obviously. Botox was a slam-dunk, but no one had clued her in.

"This one," said Rand. Surprising; his call must have ended without him telling them. They were stopped in front of the ugly Flemish forgery again. It seemed to attract you. Like a magnet.

"It's a fake," she said, before the real-estate agent could be the one to tell him.

"No *shit*," said Rand, with a punishing frown. "It's the god-damn *Garden of Earthly Delights*, for Chrissake. The original's been in the Prado since 1939." His tone hurt her feelings. Don't be so sensitive. Rand was always blunt, but it was just his style.

He turned to the agent. "If he throws this piece in, I'll pay the asking. Cash. Tomorrow."

"I don't . . . well, technically it's not for sale," the lady stumbled.

"That's the offer," said Rand. "He can take it or leave it."

Certain, unwavering. A challenge—that was Rand. Though, would she have to live with this painting? Seriously? Maybe she could get him to hang it at the office.

"It's so ugly," she protested weakly. She had to, after she'd said that to the woman.

He shot her a glance that could only be called withering.

"Guy's being extradited," he said shortly. "Did my homework."

Was that like audited? Rand hated the IRS. They were a "band of thieves." If this guy was being audited, it was all over for him. Auditing was the only thing Rand was really afraid of. Plus the SEC.

"I can certainly bring it to him," said the agent.

"Call him now," said Rand, and tapped on his own phone. He was done. That was his final word.

The lady left the room to make her call.

"Rand," she said in her kitten voice, "weren't you a teensy bit mean to me?" She sidled up to him and put her hand on his pants. He wasn't usually like that to her in front of people.

"Sweetheart," he said, not looking up from his tapping, "there's a time and a place for ignorance. Don't put it on display."

She dropped her hand.

"You need to learn to keep your mouth shut," he said. "When you're out of your depth, remember. Silence is golden."

He was in one of his moods. She left him to his tapping. She could tap too. She could shut him out just as easily. In her case it was Jelly Jump, not commodities, but shut was shut. She would not go down on him tonight. He would be lucky if he got anything.

That wasn't how you talked to your future wife. If she already had the ring, she wouldn't stand for it.

She went to the nearest bathroom, locked the door and let the tears come, holding a hand towel up to her face so that he couldn't hear. Sometimes when she cried her sobs made a hoarse scratching noise. Hiccupping . . . blunt talk can hurt, but didn't it improve you in the end? Rand said it did. Strong medicine.

That was all. He had to be honest with her, or else he couldn't be anything.

And yet . . . there was a glass bowl of seashells on the sink counter. She picked one up, stared at its parallel lines. Furrows. Straight ones that fanned out to the top, curving edge, perfectly spaced. Could it be actual nature? Or was it made in a factory?

Almost six months since she moved in with him, and still no proposal. She should have stayed at the store. She'd been fine there. She'd had a tidy routine. And Stuart had been a good guy. Not in Rand's league, but way nicer. Always nice. Stuart had never said a single mean thing. Then Rand had made a joke out of him. He started to look ridiculous. The guy who walks like a hippo? Lumbering? The one with the sloping shoulders? Woman-ish? *That's* your boyfriend? She'd had no choice but to ditch him. And be with Rand. She hadn't been able to think of him in the same way anymore. That was a bell you couldn't unring.

But Rand made her small too. At home it felt more like kidding—her ways of making up with him worked better when they were home. This had been scornful. The only difference between her and Stuart, if she was being honest, was she was hot and did things for Rand no guy could do.

Rand loved her, right? "Love you, babe." He said it all the time. But where was the evidence? It was two months ago he'd taken her to Tiffany's and she'd clearly said, *clearly* expressed her prefer-ence for the cushion-cut 11.22-karat set in platinum. Surrounded by other, tiny diamonds. He'd asked her opinion. But where was it? She held up her left hand. The finger was naked.

Her right hand bore a ring from him, he'd given her a band with rubies near the beginning. She liked it. But it didn't mean anything.

She wished she had someone to dole out advice. Her friends had slipped away after she started with him. He'd looked down on them like they were cheap. The couple of times they'd gone out and met up with *her* friends, like Cheryl and Buni, he ignored them and afterward made slighting remarks about the way they talked, their outfits. She didn't like to see them through his eyes. According to Rand, no one but him was good enough for her. It was a vote of confidence. At first she'd thought it made her amazing.

Still, she went out with them sometimes while he was busy with work. That tapered off after the time when Buni said "Rand this, Rand that, Jesus, is it Rand sitting here with us? Or is it you?"

Cheryl had looked at her sympathetically when Buni said that, but didn't stand up for her. Well, Cheryl had had a soft spot for Stuart. Afterward she said no to a couple of girls' nights out, kind of to teach them a lesson, but they just stopped calling.

She knew the answer anyway. She didn't need them to tell her. Suck it up. For the moment. When she was Mrs. she'd stand up for herself. She fixed her face.

When she came out of the bathroom, she could hear him talking in the kitchen. Was it a conference call again? She'd lurk, for now. Had to collect herself perfectly. She was almost there.

No, not a call, because the real-estate agent was talking to him.

"Of course," she said. "We can close very quickly."

Oh good! She could go in. She was so ready for this! Exciting! She'd finally done it—after weeks and weeks of seeing house after house, she'd finally found the one for them. And he was *so* picky.

"I'd like my fiancée to see it," said Rand, in a hushed, rushed voice.

That made no sense.

"Your fiancée?" asked the real-estate agent.

"I'll bring her by tomorrow, 10 a.m. To get her sign-off. Just between us," he said, still rushed and low.

". . . OK," said the lady. "Uh, yes. Sure. I can be here then."

Then, in a louder voice, Rand was talking about title companies. She didn't hear it for the rushing in her ears. Rushing like water. A waterfall of sound. Or was it blood? Blood rushing? Her knees were like water too.

The human body is 60 percent water. She learned that once. In grade school, maybe. Or even high school. Why did they teach you such dumb things? They should teach you how to read minds. At least, lie-detecting. Spies could do it, or shrinks, couldn't they? Poker players?

That's what they should teach you. Not stupid words but how to see past them.

Was there a chair?

There: the sofa. She sat on the edge of it, pulse pounding.

She couldn't have heard right. Impossible.

My fiancée. But not her. She'd already seen the house. She was right here.

She'd *been* right here. He'd made her keep the apartment, sure, he'd paid the rent, but she only went there to get her mail.

She wouldn't live in this house. It wasn't for her at all. None of them had been, none of the houses had *ever* been for her.

Just like a slap. A slap numbed you. Right now her face was numb. But later it would start hurting.

Somewhere a door slammed shut.

She was still sitting on the sofa when the real-estate agent appeared again.

"He said he had to get back to work," said the lady.

She nodded and felt her mouth stretching. Like rubber or a clown. She couldn't help it.

It wasn't fair. Not fair.

"Hey there, oh, it's OK," said the lady gently.

And sat down right beside her. An arm was around her shoulders. She must be crying again. Embarrassing. The hiccups started up. But she couldn't even care.

"Here's a tissue. Hey. It'll be OK. Not yet. I know. A shock. I know. But someday it will."

"He made me pick out a ring," she said, when she had breath again. "A cushion . . ."

She had to stop. The crying.

Had the ring been for the *other* one? Had she been basically just his personal shopper? A personal shopper and sex doll? But no, even him, he wouldn't have dared. Would he? *Dog-eat-dog world.* Maybe he'd planned it to be a surprise. Some guys presented the ring with their proposal, like at a restaurant. Tacky. A trashy idea of something fancy, like helicopter rides and single red roses on *The Bachelor.* She hoped he *had* put the ring in a champagne flute. He always said that when it came to clothes, accessories, and jewels she had excellent taste. Of course she would, since he'd found her at Barneys.

"Men like that . . . ," said the real-estate agent. She was different now, like a comforting aunt. "I've seen them before. Trust me. You wouldn't *want* to be her. Listen. She doesn't know about *you*, either. You wouldn't want to live like that, would you? You're dodging a bullet."

After a while the lady got up and came back with a glass of water. Cubes tinkling. She drank it gratefully.

Only after she drank it, she remembered the parasites. Rand
said there were parasites in tap water. Poor people drank it and
it gave them stomach worms; the worms ate all their food and
made them lazy, so then they had to ask for government hand-
outs. He always had Mercedes stock the fridge with dozens of
single-serving bottles of glacier water. Glacier water didn't have
parasites, because it came from ice and parasites didn't enjoy ice.

"I once had a relationship with an older man myself," said the
lady. "Not wealthy like Rand, but . . . anyway, the age difference
wasn't the problem. It was the power dynamic."

When she felt calm she went to the bathroom again to fix herself up. She'd still look good when she left here. Walk out like
she'd walked in. No puffy lids or eyeliner streaks.

She had some under-eye cream in her bag. She applied it.

She'd go to Rand's and take every last item she cared about,
down to her toothbrush. Down to the last shred of underwear.
Mercedes would be in the kitchen, ready to make her lunch, but
she wouldn't eat any. She didn't want lunch.

They'd ended up almost the same, Mercedes and her. Servants. Except that Mercedes would still be there tomorrow and
she would be gone.

Mercedes barely spoke English, even though she'd been here
for fifteen years. But maybe she had the right idea. Maybe it was
better, dealing with Rand, *not* to speak his language. Then you
could nod and smile and go about your business. All you had to
say was "Sí, señor." Or maybe "Yo no sé."

Well, she wouldn't talk to him anymore either. *Silence is golden*.
She would vanish like she'd never been. To him, she *would* never
have been, that was the goal. He wouldn't hear her again, he
wouldn't touch her again, he wouldn't see her again. Not even for

one second. Her superpower was invisibility. Away from him, she could let herself flicker back into sight.

Would Mercedes judge her as she crammed suitcases into the car? But Mercedes wasn't nosy and had no time to stand around watching. She actually minded her own business, did her job, stayed focused. Once during the flu Mercedes had made her soup and even sat at her bedside when Rand went out to a cocktail party . . . Leaving in such a hurry, she wouldn't have enough bags to carry all her clothes. When she got there five months ago, it all fit in just two of them. Now she'd have to take them out in armloads right on the hangers. Chanel. Dior. Valli. A few Stellas. Hell, she'd use garbage bags.

It wasn't her car, technically. He could come for it, but would he? He'd write it off. He had other cars. She drove the cheapest, probably. She'd never checked. But she suspected. A Lexus, that was all.

She exited the bathroom, putting her shoulders back. The real-estate lady wasn't around—wait, there she was. Out on the terrace, on her phone.

She passed the painting. Then stepped back in front of it. You weren't supposed to touch paintings, she knew. You had oils on your fingers, or was it salt. She hated that monster with the head of a bird. It made her grind her teeth, how much she hated it.

The rubies weren't big—no 11.22 karats. But the settings were sharp, those little claws that held each stone. She slid the ring off and held it against the bird monster's head. She pushed it in and dragged. At first, nothing, but after a bit she felt it sink in. A scratch achieved. Oh! But one of the small rubies had fallen out of her ring. She knelt and picked it up.

When she stood up again she could see the agent's back

through the glass of the French doors. The agent was divided into rectangles; an arm was in two pieces, split by a white bar.

Would the real-estate agent get in trouble? Would she get blamed for this?

No, because what could Rand say? That his other girlfriend had done it?

Anyway he wouldn't notice for a while, that was her bet. Maybe a long while. He'd be too busy remodeling. Moving in. Paying some planner from the Valley to set up his wedding.

She dug the ring into the canvas and dragged harder, scrubbed it up and down. It was tough at first soon but got easier. In the end there wasn't much to it. It might be hard to make something in the first place, but it was easy to wreck it.

She stood back and looked down at it.

You could hardly tell the bird-head thing had ever had a beak, since the tip of it was gone. Because it was in profile, without the beak it had only one big, black eye. It sat in its highchair like a baby.

Or not a baby—more like an ancient woman, a hag. A wrinkled witch with a barrel body and skinny chicken legs, dangling.

Without the beak it had no weapons. It couldn't defend itself. It was still ugly, but somehow she felt sorry for it.

Stupid. You didn't feel sorry for monsters.

SELF-EXPRESSION AND LEADERSHIP

Lynn took her to a taco stand on their first date, right near his house in East L.A. He picked her up at home and as they drove she tried to remember when she'd ever been east of the 5. In her car, sure. But had she gotten out before?

They talked about his friend Lordy, who'd tried to drown himself in a swimming pool the day they met. Later Lordy had claimed he just wanted to take a swim. He wore a fake leopard-fur hat that looked just like the hat famously worn by Mobutu Sese Seko, deceased African tyrant.

Mobutu, Lynn told her, had chosen his own name when he

came to power. It meant "the All-Powerful Warrior Who Goes from One Conquest to the Next."

He'd also renamed his whole country.

Lordy was an eccentric, besides being mentally ill—you could be both, Lynn said, two distinct categories. He always wore that style of hat: if not fake leopard fur, then fake cheetah. An orange-brown color with black spots or rings. He'd never wear real fur; he was a strict vegan. It was hell going out to eat with him because he'd ask the waitress if a dish was cooked with butter, say, and if she showed the slightest hesitation before answering he'd make her take him back to the kitchen.

Lordy was the only one of Lynn's musician friends with money. Some of it came from his records but some came from a lawsuit when he was just a kid: his parents had been killed in a collision with a semi, and there was a settlement from the trucking company. He lived with his uncle after that.

"How did he get the name Lordy?" she asked.

Lynn laughed. "Story he tells is, when he was born his mother was in so much pain giving birth all she would say was 'Lordy! Lordy!' And so that's what they named him."

Lynn had worked all over the country. Once he'd been a cook in a logging camp up in Washington—worst job he'd ever had, he said. The loggers brawled a lot and when they weren't getting into fights they spent their free time doing heroin. The upside of that was that they didn't mind him playing the drums. "When they were nodding off," he said, "I could have crashed cymbals right beside their heads. Wouldn't have bothered them a bit." He left that job to work on an industrial fishing boat, but the smell and the guts got to him. And the confined spaces. Plus he couldn't play.

Then he came back home to take care of his sick father, and after that he stayed. He'd gotten an education degree and worked as a high-school teacher until Lordy, whose uncle lived in Lynn's neighborhood, heard him drumming and asked him to play on his new album. He still taught, but now he also had the band.

He didn't want her to have to wait in line for the tacos. He asked her what she wanted as they stood in front of the board, then found them a table, a nice, shady one beside a big hedge of bougainvillea. It was a plastic table but it had a homey checked cloth on it, and there were festive lights in the trees, Christmas lights in the shape of chili peppers. Corona signs and all the rest. Negra Modelo. It was mostly families eating.

His home turf. She liked that he'd brought her here.

It was so easy talking to him she had to remind herself they didn't have much in common. His chest and shoulders bore a tattoo of a cherry tree, branches with white-petaled blossoms stretching over them. She'd seen it at the pool. He was practically a giant: he towered over her and had to weigh twice as much. She tried to picture it—was missionary out of the question, or could he hold himself up on his elbows? But that would be like weightlifting. On the other hand, men were used to it. Weren't they?

The tacos were good but greasy. You really needed the napkins. If she ate these things all the time, she'd look like the mamas one table over. Worse actually, since they looked good a little plump. And seemed happy. Most people seemed happy in restaurants. Or the right restaurants, anyway. Sitting around tables, eating and drinking under the twinkling strings of light. The women at the next table laughed and nodded as they ate, surrounded by children. Skinny was more of a white obsession, Lynn had said in a text. She hoped she wasn't too skinny for him. She had the top shelf, anyway. She'd always had that. Maybe it worked in her favor. What was that song? In heavy rotation a while back. "I ain't no size two / But I can shake it shake it like I'm supposed to do."

It was sung by a white girl. Kind of pretending to be black. She hadn't been skinny to begin with. But she would be soon. Hell, probably already, since she had hits. When they got rich and famous they got skinny, if they weren't already. Clockwork. There were hardly any exceptions.

After they finished eating Lynn drove her to his house, the one he'd grown up in. A modest stucco two-story, but attractive. There was a motorcycle parked in the driveway with a cover on it. It had been his father's and he hardly ever drove it, he said. Just every now and then when he was restless. "You know those hazy days, when no branch is moving and the city feels airless?" he said. "I hate that airless feeling. I like to feel the wind."

His drums were set up in the basement. There was also a keyboard, a bunch of other equipment, records and speakers all around. An old couch was pushed against the wall—old but clean-looking. "The room is soundproofed now, but it didn't used to be. I used to bug the shit out of the neighbors. But on the other hand, if I hadn't gotten on their nerves, Lordy would never have found me." She noticed the posters—*Power to the People*, one said, showing a raised fist.

"Listen to this," he said, and put on a song, kind of folksy. She was surprised, but she liked it. Then he took out a vinyl album. "Here's an older version of it," he said, and put the needle down. "It was originally written in the nineteenth century. A workers' anthem."

She sat down on the couch and sank in: it must have broken

springs. The song was like a hymn, or at least a choral thing, because it was lots of voices together. *Arise, ye prisoners of starvation, / Arise, ye wretched of the earth.*

Lynn came over and sat next to her while they listened. His presence, like him, was huge. But gentle. Wouldn't he do anything, touch her leg? Put an arm around her shoulders? Maybe he didn't like her. The simplest explanation . . . what was that saying? The simplest explanation was usually the right one. She didn't want to think about it, in that case, but the question was distracting. She let her eyes rest on the wall—that old fake-wood paneling made out of what, vinyl? She should know, but none of her houses ever had it. She only remembered it from the late seventies, from when she was a little kid. A framed gold record hung there with a brass plaque and some words beneath. She couldn't read them from here.

"That was my father's," said Lynn. "He was a singer. Soul music. The Motown sound. He had the one record. Never made much from it. Old story, the label ripped him off. Then—family to raise. That record was his moment of glory."

Behold them seated in their glory / The kings of mine and rail and soil . . .

"Glory," repeated Lynn. He'd said it, and then the song did.

What *was* glory? She didn't know. She didn't know at all. It had to do with shining, she thought. Or living on in memory. *Glory, glory hallelujah.* Her mother had been religious, but only went to church when she was sad. It must not have helped, because after that was when she locked herself in her bedroom and they had to forage for food. Even, sometimes, go next door or across the street for it. A box of cereal or some bread. The neighbors had stepped up, the ones whose house she remembered because it had *The Joy of Sex* in the bathroom. And orange shag carpeting. She didn't have their names anymore. But when her mother was locked in, sometimes she and her little sister had slept in the neighbors' guest bedroom. Gotten warm meals, mac and cheese from a box.

The neighbors didn't call Child Protective Services, but always took care of them at those times and said their mother would pull through. It was too much for their mother. She tried, but she couldn't handle it. The world was too much, their mother said. *Can you not feel the pain of everyone?* she once asked, very serious, holding Nina by the shoulders and looking into her eyes. *Can you feel the pain that resides in all beings?*

Nina was only eight then. She tested by waiting for a minute to see if the pain came, but kept feeling the same as usual. So finally she said, *Um, I don't* think *I can.*

Her mother turned away, disappointed. Dropped her hands. Not disappointed, that was too mild. More like crushed.

They'd had a rabbit that died because—she thought but didn't know for sure—her mother had forgotten to feed it. When it died, shivering in the corner of the cage all skin and bones, she had sobbed. Her mother had too. Longer than her and Marnie by far.

Her mother had sung, warbling: *Mine eyes have seen the glory of the coming of the Lord.*

"Hey," said Lynn. "Are you OK?"

"Sorry," she said. "Just thinking about my family."

He didn't pry. Relief, since she wasn't up for talking about it. Especially she wasn't up for talking about the death. Bad thought; block it. You're on a date. Don't be such a Debbie Downer, Marnie used to say. Once Marnie had been the cheerful one, always capering and making faces to distract her, when they were kids. Maybe that was why she was so angry now—maybe, as the older sister, *she* should have been the one making faces.

"You don't have to do that," said Lynn. "I can tell a real smile from a fake one. I know what we'll do. We'll dance."

"Oh. I'm a really bad dancer," she said.

"Hell, I know that. You're white, aren't you? Let's do it anyway."

"But not to this," she said. The last strains of the workers' anthem were already fading.

He got up and lifted the needle, switched to an MP3 player.

Aaaaaow! Say it now! I'm back!

"Everybody knows this," he said.

He reached out a hand and pulled her up.

"Get up offa that thing," he talked along with it. "And dance till you feel better."

So they did, and she did. He held her hand the whole time, which made it easier. He swung her around and twirled her until she stumbled and laughed. First she'd thought he was so forbidding, but now—it was kindness that emanated from him.

They went upstairs, into the air-conditioning, when they were sweaty from dancing. He poured her a glass of wine. He wouldn't have any himself because he had to drive her home. You couldn't drive, drink and be black all at once, he added. It overloaded the system.

She hoped he wouldn't take her home too soon. The wine was warm in her mouth and she sipped it slowly; the glass gave her hand something to do.

He toured her past a staircase of family pictures, showed her the faces and said who they were. His father, now deceased, his mother, deceased even before the father—Latina, she saw, explaining his lighter skin. If he were as dark as his father, the tattoo wouldn't even show up on him. Would it? There were five brothers and sisters, a couple half-, he said. One full brother, one full sister. They mostly lived nearby. One had problems—his brother had been in and out of jail. Possession raps. They were still close. They helped each other when they could.

"I have a sister, but she moved to Texas," she told him. "I haven't seen her in years. She always seems to get so mad at me. I can't do anything right. It's because, I guess, she doesn't think I protected her enough. When we were young. I was the older one. Before the last time I saw her she went to this—I don't know, self-empowerment-type lecture? Or motivational speaking? And after that she wasn't as nice to me. Things are my fault, she thinks. And maybe they were. I can't remember. I tried to say sorry."

She'd said sorry for everything. For whatever she'd ever done or not done, she *was* sorry. Being sorry was easy. She had no trouble believing things were her fault, at least partly. But no matter what she said, Marnie didn't want to hear it. She wanted something else. She wanted Nina to go to the same empowerment lecture series she attended. Some company offered them, a pyramid scheme maybe—you paid a bit at first, and later it was more.

Until she took the course, Marnie had said, she wasn't *in the conversation*.

"But I'm right here," she'd protested. "I'm *in* the conversation. Aren't we having it?"

"You're not enrolled," said Marnie. "You can't speak to my listening."

Nina had offered to pay for lunch; she couldn't stand to do the math over who'd ordered a seltzer and who drank tap. But Marnie had shaken her head, asked for the bill and painstakingly separated the items they'd both eaten, down to the last nickel. She said Nina couldn't buy her off.

It was as though, when Marnie looked at her, she was seeing a different person. She didn't look often; she tended to avoid eye contact. But when she did, it was with suspicion, like Nina was covered in some version of the past she herself didn't recognize. It made her feel trapped. She'd never been told the nature of her crimes, so she couldn't defend herself. They used to be inseparable: when they were girls they were joined at the hip. Had to be, because most of the time it had been just the two of them. And somewhere in there, without wanting to, she must have hurt her sister.

You didn't know the harms you did.

"You don't need to say sorry so much," said Lynn. Unlike Marnie he looked her right in the eyes. He did like her—didn't he?

But he didn't take her upstairs. He turned and headed down to the kitchen again, and she followed. Her wineglass was empty.

"You want one more, a nightcap before we go?" he asked. He'd noticed the empty glass. He paid attention. And yet he didn't move toward her.

Maybe she was supposed to make the first move. But she couldn't stand to. She might have it all wrong.

"You think I'm a lush, don't you," she said, as they went back into the kitchen. Half-joking. Half-insecure. More insecure.

"I think you're beautiful," said Lynn, and turned and held her face and kissed her.

Then he let her go.

"Now for that second glass," he said. "Lush."

On the way home she sat on the passenger side feeling so happy it was hard to speak normally, casually. She was tempted to put her arm around the back of the driver's seat, but then— there was a tinge of presumption to that gesture. She never knew what to do in a passenger seat. In her job she was always the one driving. Often the clients sat in the back, so that she felt like a chauffeur. She *was* a chauffeur. She fiddled with the straps on her bag.

"Can I see you again?" asked Lynn, in front of her duplex. He'd walked her to the door holding her hand.

"Yes, please," she said.

"Soon?"

"As soon as you like."

"I like tomorrow."

"I like it too."

Inside, she felt herself spilling out. Or over. She didn't have the right words. Were there good words for it? There was only time, speeding up. Time spiraling. Or no, that couldn't be—that was a wrong idea.

Maybe it was just that she felt herself moving through time, for once. You went along at the same pace for so long that it felt like you were standing still; then something shifted and suddenly life was rushing past. Not in the sense of disappearing, but in the sense of happening. She was in her house, and others were in theirs, and now she knew she was one of all of them. She was one bee in one cubby in a honeycomb. Or one star in a constellation. A thousand points of light, someone had said. But there were far more than that.

Was it just that when you felt like this, you felt the world wanted you, for once? Was that why everyone was obsessed with it?

One person *was* the world.

She wanted to run. Should she run into her house?

She bounded into the living room, where the overhead light was blazing. She spun around, arms flung out. Not as good as dancing. Just as she was slowing down the doorbell rang.

Oh no. Was it him? Had he seen her?

Maybe she shouldn't answer it. But then, if it was him . . . whoever it was had to have seen her run and spin. How would she explain it?

If it was him, maybe she wouldn't need to.

She went to the door, a knot in her stomach. It was dark. It was late.

"Who's there?" she called.

No answer. Then again, the door was thick. She wished it had a peephole, but the landlord was too cheap.

But what if it *was* him?

She clicked on the porch light. That way any potential assailant might have a witness: the next-door neighbor who smoked on his stoop at night.

She opened it.

The chain-smoker's wife. Phew. She held a pile of mail.

"Delivered to our box again," she said. "It looks like mostly junk, but still."

"It's always mostly junk," said Nina, and took it.

She had a home health business, this woman. If you had allergies and were a New Age type, you went to her and she pressed glass vials of foods against your skin. Right through the glass, supposedly your body reacted to them, telling you to avoid soy or gluten. Surprisingly, she had numerous customers.

It was the smoking husband who had explained it to Nina. He wasn't a New Ager; he worked in construction. He said the allergy testing was bullshit. "Snake oil. Pure quackery. But it keeps me in these," he joked, raising his crumpled pack of Marlboros.

"But she believes it, right?" Nina had asked. "She's not ripping them off on purpose, is she?"

"One hundred percent," nodded the husband.

She hadn't been sure what that meant.

But now she wanted to know. Did the wife believe in what she did?

"Can I ask you a question?" she said.

"Sure," said the woman. Surprised, maybe. Still friendly though.

"Your practice," said Nina. "The allergy testing. Does it depend on science? Or, like, belief?"

"Oh, science," said the woman, and smiled. "One hundred percent."

Nina thanked her and closed the door.

She stood without moving then: what if she did what Marnie wanted, went to the self-help group? It was *all* Marnie wanted. It was the only thing she'd asked of her. If she went—Marnie had told her they held "seminars" in every major city—maybe she'd have a sister again. Was it so hard? She should have done it sooner. She'd been afraid it was cultish, but it wasn't like you lived in a guarded compound. You didn't have to sleep with the leader or be a sister wife. You paid money and went to meetings, that was all, at some big hotel or conference center, and wore a nametag, and after the meetings were over you went home. Even if she couldn't stand it, if it was like a hair shirt she had to wear, it would be worth it. Worth every penny.

Because Marnie would have to talk to her again, if she went. She wouldn't have any excuses left.

She'd look online for it. Right now. She'd sign up. Whatever it took. Just give in.

Joy made you look foolish, if you showed it. Always she thought of what her mother said—pain brimmed in everything that lived. Hands on her shoulders, fingers pinching hard but not cruelly.

She'd understood it back then, even, in her kid's way that didn't put words to the feeling: the pinch was not cruel, just desperate. Her mother wanted her to see. Pain was electric, flowing from one to many or many to one, a current that moved among them.

But so was joy.

Can you feel the pain that resides in all beings?

What would she say to her mother now?

No, Mama. And neither could you. The pain you felt was all your own.

Joy was ambient, a charge in the atmosphere. What you could do was partake. Some people didn't have a choice, she knew that too well. Some got mostly pain instead.

Pretend her mother hadn't taken the pills. Pretend they hadn't both failed Marnie, pretend that Marnie cherished her still, looked up to her with the old childlike devotion. Pretend her mother and little sister had stayed at home, taken care of each other while she'd gone off to school. Gotten the education she wanted. Seen the wide world. Pretend all that: who might she be? How different?

Who knew?

One thing was sure: still electric. Still a pulse in a deep field of stars.

THE FALL OF BERLIN

She loved her home so much, had loved it so deeply for so many years, that when she thought of her death it was the house she felt sorry for.

No one would ever hold this place as dear as she did. The house wasn't grand—from the outside it was frankly plain. But she'd furnished it so deliberately, so delicately over time that every shade of color or light, every nook and corner was cared for, warm and welcoming. *Curated*, they said now, about everything. Her home was curated.

The furnishings were only her belongings and not permanent by nature, though she wished them to be. On the news recently a venerable archaeologist in Syria had been murdered by militants.

He'd been defending a cache of ancient artifacts from Palmyra, refusing to tell the radicals where they were. They cut his head off. When she heard it on the news she cried.

Courage, she thought. That was courage.

But this was only a home, only her house, and even before she died the whole place would be taken apart methodically, no sentiment wasted. Her chairs, rugs, lamps would be separated from each other with violent haste, never again to be a part of this perfect harmony. If she was lucky they would be sold to people who valued them. That was the best case, and even the best case was unbearable.

She gazed out the window from her favorite armchair— a graceful prospect. In the breeze her front yard trees dipped and swayed. The greatest of them was a Norfolk Island pine, its rounded needles like velvet. Beyond the moving bough she could see a haze of blue lupines among the river rocks, and then the neighbors' hedge. Beyond the hedge was only sky, where, on this sunlit late afternoon, a bank of cumulus had gathered. Billowing flowers of atmosphere.

Now was the time to give up what she loved. She knew that. But it was so *hard*. She should have specialized in Buddhists instead of fascists, then maybe she'd be ready for the world to fall away. Ready to rise, her arms outstretched, with nothing to the left of her and nothing to the right. Enter the air.

There was his car, its top a hard shine of silver, pulling up to the curb. It wouldn't be assisted living, at least—for this she was gladder than she could ever say. Her son's guesthouse was butter-colored stucco and surrounded by a lush garden. He paid a gardener to do the heavy lifting, but she would putter around, prune and put in some plantings here and there. She would dwell in the backyard quiet and humble, the troll lady in the hut, the gnome in the hollyhocks. The grandmother in the calla lilies. Twice over, for her new daughter-in-law, the twenty-four-year-old he'd left his first wife and his son for, was expecting.

There were three boxes, all marked *Study*. Before her hip went bad she would have had the boxes neatly stacked in the front hall, waiting, but now it was virtually impossible for her to carry them. They sat through the open door to the study, in her line of sight: *Study. Study. Study.* Betrayed by joints! In the end, it came down to parts. This load was a small one, only art. The earliest moment of moving, the nonessentials—nothing she needed to sit or sleep or eat on. But things that mattered, all the same.

"Mom?"

She'd never liked that word. Preferred *Mama, Mother*, even *Mommy*. When he was little he'd called her those, but it changed to *Mom* over time—greater neutrality. More masculine.

His head came around the doorjamb.

"Where's the stuff?"

She inclined her head toward the study door.

"These three? That's it?"

"For now. I'm just going to look at the wall space today, see where the pieces should go."

He lifted the first box, walked out the door.

"Thank you," she called after. She wished she could do it herself. Wishes had to be surrendered. *Surrender*, she thought, *give up*, these were verbs of defeat.

But at the end of things, surrender was the only victory.

Maudlin. She wasn't dying yet, for Chrissake, just moving out, which people did every day. Commonplace. No hospital smells in store for her, no cafeteria smells, no humiliation in the loss of privacy. She'd visited her cousin at an old folks' home. Upscale, they claimed, but the smells had been so disgusting. Also the tube lights overhead, that sick fluorescence that bleached out the world.

He was helping her out of the armchair next, and she was performing her invalid's walk toward the front door. Once she was up or down it was fine—the pain was in the transitions. Sometimes she was able to convince herself that in the act of slow, deliberate walking she was maintaining her dignity; other times she felt like a wreck. A stately wreck, she insisted to herself hopefully, like a ghost ship moving across the wide ocean: its sails were tattered, but proudly it faced the wind.

Or she might look like a trash barge. Hard to know.

It was just fifteen minutes' drive and on the way he talked on his cell phone. She got to hear both sides of the conversation— sports team opinions she didn't care to follow—since he was driving and had it hooked up to the audio. Why he needed such a large SUV was a mystery to her. She'd always assumed these hulking cars were mostly for obese people.

"Lora will help you, OK?" he asked as he parked, finally done reeling off his commentary on sports scores. "I have to go pick up Jeremy after I drop your boxes in back. He's actually coming over tonight. His first time since, you know."

Poor kid. And yet: one day the acne would be gone.

He disappeared around the side of the house carrying the first box and she made her labored way to the front door, which was unlocked. Then she was moving—trundling, as she thought of it—into the main house, expecting an interception but also indifferent to it. The place's benign and subtly sculpted appointments looked like a page from a West Elm catalog. Too much off-white,

the default palette of many a modern homeowner . . . an error of
domestic engineering. There was no surer way to make a house
feel cold and generic than by painting its insides white.

She always puzzled over the place's décor elements, probably
bought from the selfsame West Elm or another such bourgeois
home-furnishings vendor, possibly meant to conjure a faint idea
of art. For instance, here in the large foyer—more like a lux-
ury hotel lobby—there were life-size, stylized brown branches
along one wall, made not of wood but of plastic. Or metal. Or
plastic painted to look like metal. On another wall there were
large autumn leaves in shadow boxes. But neither her son nor her
daughter-in-law had an interest in trees or leaves. Paul had told
her more than once that a garden, to him, was nothing but added
property value.

Farther along she passed a floating shelf made out of cut-up
books. The books had been disassembled and covered in shellac
or something, maybe epoxy, all glued together with their spines
pointing outward. *Scouting for Boys. Birds and Beasts of Africa.
Pig-Sticking or Hog-Hunting. Sport in War. Paddle Your Own
Canoe.* Baden-Powell, if she wasn't mistaken. The famed Boy
Scout founder. Also, fascist.

On the shelf sat glass globes with ferns sticking out of them.

At times she thought she should have been an interior decora-
tor instead of a scholar. She would have failed, needless to say: too
many harsh judgments. She would have tried to rule her clients
instead of satisfy them, ride roughshod over their taste. Correct,
uplift and educate. She would have been as popular as head lice.

No wonder she'd thrown in her lot, instead, with the Nazis.

On the cream-colored sectional sat Lora, reading a pregnancy book that had the heft of an annotated King James. They

put them through their paces these days, the wealthy mothers. You had to read a Bible-sized parenting manual—and make no mistake, its commandments were stern. *Thou shalt not eat unpasteurized cheese.* Lora looked up, smiled sweetly—a good-natured girl, despite being a trophy—and stood, offering a wide array of beverages, up to and including a fine Hendrick's G&T.

But she couldn't stop walking now on her way to the guesthouse. No. Her progress would not be impeded.

"You know what it's like," she told Lora, who had stood up and padded nervously beside her, belly leading. One hand hovered midair, as though to prop her up in the event of a sudden timber. "Once I go down, I can't get up again. *I've fallen and I can't get up.* Remember that? The famous commercial?"

The girl shook her head, confused. Of course. That commercial was before her time. Born in 1991. Literally half the age of the man she was married to. Paul was already forty-eight, but still didn't believe in old age. As far as he was concerned, decrepitude was something that happened to others. His mother, for instance.

It would come as quite a shock when it happened to him. At that point he'd have to marry a twelve-year-old to feel young.

"Let me get it," said Lora, and opened the door for her. She stepped onto the deck, slowly down the redwood stairs, slowly onto the flagstone path. The garden was beautiful, though it lacked her Norfolk Island pine. It lacked her lupines and swells of California poppies . . . but those could easily be ushered in. Her pine, though—she'd never see its like again. Once she moved here, after her own dear house was sold away, no tree she planted would grow tall before she disappeared.

She'd take that G&T, she told Lora as soon as she was situated in the guesthouse on a chair—thank you. Lora kept up a stream of quiet talk as they made their way down the path to the cottage, whose door stood open now; Paul had deposited her boxes square in the middle of the doorway, she could see, so that she'd have to steer around them. Lora said something about a stroller, then a swing, then a vibrating chair.

Containers. Babies were mostly about buying polymers now. Feminism had taken the form of plastic. Arms are the best place for babies, she wanted to say, you don't need all that crap.

In the small house it was cool and a fan turned slowly on the ceiling. Lora was surprisingly patient about holding up the pieces of framed art against the walls. She marked the walls carefully with a pencil once she was told where a piece should go.

"What's this one of?" she asked. Remarkable image, shades of red, a golden amber, steel-gray in the background. "Oh wow. Is that black thing a . . . ?"

"Swastika, yes," she said. "This is an original poster for the most famous of all the Nazi propaganda films. By Leni Riefenstahl. You've heard of it, I'm sure. *Triumph of the Will*?"

"You're not afraid the swastika will, like, offend someone?"

"Offend," she murmured. The girl made her shake her head inwardly, but she couldn't help liking her. "Well, it's what I studied. Study. Still working on a paper or two. It's not an *endorsement*, dear. I had these pieces in my office, you see. They're part of my work—the art and the propaganda of fascism. The aesthetics."

Maybe Paul had omitted to tell Lora that detail, how most of their relatives had perished in the Gulag.

She wouldn't put it past him. He was a guy with little time for history, even his own family's.

Offend. She'd have her desk here—she'd re-create her study in miniature. She couldn't walk well, but she could still write.

"That soldier looks like he's holding the flag so awkwardly," said Lora. "It's weird how high his elbow is."

The elbow *was* notably high.

"Well, bearing the standard of the thousand-year Reich wasn't a task for pansies," she told Lora. Though technically, of course, it often had been.

"I like *this* one a lot," said the girl, taking the next framed poster from the box. "He's handsome. And the baby's so cute!"

Indeed: a distinguished gray-mustached gentleman was holding up a baby against a blue sky.

"That's Joseph Stalin," she said.

She said it kindly, she thought. Not condescending, she hoped. Just letting her know.

But the name didn't ring a bell. Lora smiled and nodded, as though a distant but welcome relation had been introduced. "I *adore* how they dressed old-fashioned babies in these lacy outfits, don't you? I saw one picture from like eighteen-something where even though it was a boy, it wore a long white dress." She held up Stalin near the door to the kitchenette. "You could put it right here! The baby's flowers and that little flag go with the colors of the backsplash tiles, don't they?"

She heard herself sigh softly. Lately she'd been sighing a lot. It was a medical syndrome, among other things. She'd looked it up.

"It has to go over the desk, like the other. For now, maybe—I don't want to press my luck, but do you think possibly—that gin and tonic you mentioned . . . ?"

"Oh wow, of course," said Lora. "Pregnancy brain. Sorry. I'll be right back."

Once she was installed, she'd have her own wet bar. She depended on the cocktail hour, felt actual tenderness on its approach—every day, a grateful expectation. When it came to alcohol, you couldn't afford to be at someone else's mercy.

With Lora gone she could soak in the mood of the place. It was three rooms plus a bathroom, not too small, and many windows—the rear ones, off the kitchen and bedroom, had a view of the tennis club over the fence. The beige of its buildings in the background; in the foreground a red expanse of clay court.

"They're playing foosball," said Lora. She came in holding the tumbler. "Paul and Jeremy."

Last time she checked, the boy still hadn't been speaking to Lora. His policy had been straightforward when it came to his stepmother: silence. She was only eight years his senior. He spoke to her mostly in monosyllables. Barely spoke to his father either. His mother was deeply depressed, so it was scarcely a surprising resentment, but all in all, Lora—who'd been ignorant of Paul's first marriage when he first picked her up at a nightclub, due to outright lies on his part, and then had gotten knocked up—accepted it with good grace.

"So when are you thinking you'll move in?" asked Lora.

"I'm not in a hurry," she told her. She took a sip of her drink and let it sit on her tongue.

"Paul's going to feel so much better once you're here with the au pair. I repainted the east suite for her. Like, robin's-egg blue? I'll show you later."

"It's good of you."

"I love that she'll help you out but also double as a nanny! So great! Right?"

"So great."

The Swedish au pair would be changing diapers at the bookends of life, from Huggies to Depends. No, stop, too harsh, she wasn't there yet—so far, at least, incontinence wasn't her lot. Still. The au pair was a nursing student and six feet tall, Lora said, with big hands; she'd be nice enough but likely condescending as she managed the helpless, both newborn and ancient.

Paul wanted her to move soon. He claimed he was afraid of a hip breaking when she was alone in her house, no one nearby to notice or help . . . though something had rung false when he said that, come to think of it. Since when was he *afraid* of her poor health? He noticed even her hospital stays in passing, at best. Maybe he was just embarrassed by the prospect of her keeling over, being found like an upside-down beetle, limbs helplessly pedaling. He set great store by appearances, her son. He'd been embarrassed by the sight of human weakness since he was a teenager. And she was a poster child for weakness now, any idiot could see it. But maybe she underestimated him: maybe *she* was the one who should feel ashamed of casting aspersions on the nobility of her child's feelings—a bad habit of hers, taking cheap shots. Privately, even. There was nothing funny about that eighties medical device commercial, for instance, just common stupidity. The sterile humor of mockery.

Easy mockery: it clung to the mind like a spider.

He wanted her to move, but to move she would have to destroy her home.

"You just relax," said Lora. "I'll send one of the guys to get you when dinner's ready. We'll eat on the deck. OK?"

After Lora had gone back to the kitchen she sat on the patio in front of the guesthouse sipping her drink. Could have used another jigger, but it was nice enough. The sunset's pink bands were partly hidden by the trees that rose around the edges of the property, tall trees like oak and eucalyptus. She liked the trees, but she would miss having a wider view of the sky.

When Jeremy came to get her, walking his slouching walk, his lowrider jeans a mere hair's breadth from exposure of his genitals, he wore his default sullen expression. But he grinned when she held out her glass to him. Only the watery dregs. He was well below drinking age so he appreciated even the smallest gestures toward inebriation. She made it her business, when not in view of either of his parents, to parcel out booze to him. Gin was better than marijuana, after all, when it came to conversation.

"Thanks, Gram," he said, and slugged it back. "You rule."

He set the empty glass on the rim of a planter and bent down to help her up. He was a perceptive kid, despite the crude acting out. She saw the bad behavior as a tithe, not to a church but to his pubescent demographic. He'd grow out of it. Meanwhile he knew just the right angle, just the right speed at which to help raise her to her feet, and the pressure of his hands was solid and comfortable, unlike his father's. Paul always had a more important place to be and didn't pay much attention; usually he jerked her out of her chair so abruptly it made her bones rattle.

Sure, her grandson liked her mostly because she slipped him liquor, but she could hardly blame him for that.

Ahead she saw the deck table with places set for dinner—those massively oversized goblets. They were so trendy now you could barely buy anything else to drink your red from. Some pompous ass had told the foodies their wine was only acceptable when served in fishbowls with narrow sticks on the bottom; well, they got their comeuppance when they had to tip the things almost vertical to eke out the last sip. She'd once seen a hedge-fund manager, some obnoxious colleague of Paul's, break the upper rim of a giant goblet on his nose in the middle of a buffoonish anecdote about a "slutty girl." Served him right.

She'd chortled loudly and perhaps a shade too long for good manners; Paul had covered his embarrassment by implying she was senile.

She could have made a retort, but a mother spared her son, when it was in her power to do so. It had been her choice.

In the low wind of twilight paper napkins were fluttering, pinned down by cutlery. Cloth napkins would never occur to Lora. She might have seen some white ones in a restaurant once.

The sun was throwing shadows against the wall of the house. She leaned on Jemmy, whose arm was thin but strong. Yesterday he'd been bouncing in a swing, chubby and angelic. Now tall and pimpled and rangy, with the ass-crack-revealing jeans and an addiction to pot and masturbation.

But he was a good boy.

She hoped the new baby was a girl, though, had to admit she hoped she'd have a granddaughter this time around. In the long run, less heartbreak. Because boys, and later men, regardless of their best intentions often seemed to yearn for something they just never succeeded in defining. You pitied them for it, your heart went out to them, but still there was a chronic gap between what they should be and what they were capable of being.

Into that gap civilization fell.

Not that Lora was much different, in terms of her net effect. The footprint of Lora on the earth. A hostess at the nightclub now. Made less there than the au pair would cost. They didn't work just for room and board these days. Frankly, she suspected Paul didn't trust Lora by herself with a baby. She was warm, so nice you felt guilty, and full of just about nothing. For her it wasn't that history had faded but that it had never existed to begin with.

To a child the world began anew every day. All life was the life

of the self, the life of now, and stories flitted around the margins
like butterflies.

But at least, unlike Paul, Lora did no harm.

Could that be said for her? In old age and weakness, was all
forgiven? Did it need to be?

What had she done with her whole life? She'd studied them.
The ones who took her parents, grandparents, aunts and uncles.
Her baby sister. The ones who took so many. And after all it was
the United States they'd wanted to imitate: these easy-living,
these complacent and iniquitous United States. Hitler admired,
with deepest faith, the way the New World conquerors had so
effectively wreaked genocide upon the Indians. Established the
supremacy of whites. That recent study—what had it said? She
kept up, even if she wasn't a contender anymore. There might
have been about 80 million of them. Not 8 million, as early
twentieth-century scholars used to guess. As many as *80 million*, it
was now estimated by the archaeologists, the demographers who
worked on historic population densities. Cabeza de Vaca, Lewis
and Clark, their stories of the Indians they met so frequently, the
size of the country. That meant the genocide in the Americas had
taken maybe 10 million, at the low end—60 million at the high.

The greatest genocide of all had happened *here*. War and foreign
disease, spread purposefully, often. Enslavement had failed, with
the Indians. They'd rather die than work the fields. Mostly they'd
been nomads, of course. They didn't care for the white man's land-
work. So Africans had to be imported, for the purpose of enslavement, because the Indians didn't make good slaves. Hell, they
didn't make even mediocre ones. The red man was no slave at all.
They had refused to farm and been summarily erased, and other
unfortunates had been brought in. Under the whip, the black man
agreed to work the fields. For a time.

But who spoke of the Indians? Where was it mentioned?

In academic journals, that was where. Indian news. A handful of native activists. No one listened to them. There was a founding myth, and their petty quibbles existed only at the margins.

And what had she done? She'd studied the art and design of the imitators. The second or even third generation. The weak-minded copiers of race domination, with their brilliant banners and their engineers of empire. She'd scrutinized their accoutrements. Following in their path with a microscope and a sad flutter of little-read articles. *This* was the song she offered up to the fallen?

She'd held it as an article of faith that distance gave you insight. But distance gave you distance.

She would have laughed at herself, if she had it in her.

Something faltered, a pang shot up her leg from the knee. Flicker of agony. She clutched Jemmy's arm harder.

"Gram! You OK?"

"I think—"

There it was again, a long stab up to the joint of the hip. To the bursa, that sack in the joint, full of fluid. She'd had shots in that sack, steroid shots when she was younger, a giddy girl in her late sixties. They never helped. Her whole leg was folding. She had the feeling she was hollow: what bones she had were made of glass. But terribly, the glass was sharp on each end, split into shards like a paintbrush whose bristles were pins. And those pins were embedded in the nerve-wracked flesh.

Jemmy spun and was standing in front of her, clasping her around the waist. Bearing her full weight, must be. She sagged but didn't hit the flagstones. A high, panicky voice came to her ears.

"Aleska? Aleska!"

Vaguely she remembered asking Lora to call her "Professor Korczak," though. But could she have? Possibly? Or was that a dream? She hoped so. She couldn't have been so rude. She was rigorous, but rude only when provoked. Not to the innocent; it hadn't been her upbringing. The true people of the book were seldom impolite.

The young woman was running toward her. Worried! Poor dear. Not so fast, she wanted to say. You'll hurt the embryo. Wasn't that what they called it?

"Gram, can you hear me? Can you understand what I'm saying?"

She was unsure. Her bones were rubber or they were spiky. They couldn't hold.

The weakness receded as suddenly as it had come on.

"I'm OK. Thanks, Jemmy. Thanks, dear. Please—just give me a moment."

"Steady there, Gram."

"It was just my—was my body."

"You're OK, Gram."

Still a bit confused. A form of aphasia, possibly. Where you say the wrong thing. But she felt firmer and steadier every second. She was solid. She was herself. For a little while yet.

"I *am* OK. Yes. I'm quite all right now. My apologies."

"Aleska, are you—what was that? You want to sit down? Rest?"

The girl's pretty, concerned face was suspended beside them. Jemmy still held her up. He was the solid one; he was the mainstay. She thought of his mother, an intelligent woman, if depressive. Worlds apart, the first wife and the second: a woman and then a girl. Paul knew the difference—even he knew. But for his purposes he didn't give a shit.

It made her sad. She'd wanted to raise a finer man.

"I'll make it to the table," she told them. Paul was coming out the back door finally.

"She stumbled," Lora called to him. "But it was almost like she was having an attack or something."

"I'm all right now," she repeated faintly.

She felt like an ancient bride, advancing along the garden path on Jeremy's arm toward the wedding feast. He'd give her away. But to whom? She was already given. She *had* given. She'd given all she had. And it was surely not enough.

Not by a long shot.

In so many traditions, heaven was in the sky. It made sense—up there where personhood dissolved, dominion of light and ether.

Go on, just leave the earth. Your work here is done. Insufficient. But over with.

But how much she loved this place.

If only she could find someone to live in her home exactly as it was, not with its insides stripped away but with everything still in position, soft and careful, its every corner well-disposed to company. If someone could exist there, on through time, and quietly appreciate the place the way she had—if they could know the small, unsayable beauties of that cherishment. In all their singular detail. If she could hand that down inside her house.

I may have failed, but I knew one precious thing: I knew what was beautiful.

So take my home, here, take the way I lived, nestled within these rolling hills. Take my view of the sky, and on a clear day the ocean.

You too will thank this life. Flooded with gratefulness. Bow your head.

THE MEN

You could almost call them a squad—sometimes as many as seven, when they all pitched in. They were reliable for plumbing, basic carpentry, minor electrical fixes, and digging holes. They liked to dig holes. They liked it a lot. Twice she'd ordered a bunch of seedlings for the backyard just to keep them busy.

The men'll take care of it, she'd say to herself, if she had a lot on her to-do list, and sooner or later the men would file in. Their blunt-fingered hands were capable of surprising dexterity.

They were smaller than midgets but larger than cats—about the size of dachshunds, if the doxies were walking on their hind legs. They'd smile sometimes. But not often. They played their cards close to the vest. The men weren't much for talking.

She wasn't sure where they went on their own time, though once she'd found them hunkered down around the TV staring slack-jawed at a game. And she'd walked past them grilling steaks one afternoon. They were using the old indoor/outdoor George Foreman, on its stand in the driveway. She hadn't seen it since Dan left. She didn't mind.

"Hey, those look good," she said.

One of them shrugged.

She always got the feeling they preferred her to move along. No chitchat, please. Almost a precondition of their service. It was all right. Honestly, what did she have in common with them? The answer was nothing. The men didn't do small talk. Mostly they disappeared after a set of tasks was done and reappeared for the next.

They were small, but not elfin. When she tried to think of them as helper elves—like the ones in fairy tales, say, who cut leather and stitched it into handmade shoes during the night to help a humble cobbler—it made her laugh. They were dachshund-sized, sure, but very solid. They were burly, and walked with a swagger. They didn't dance nimbly or wear pointy caps.

When Dan left she'd gotten depressed. She'd been blindsided, after all. No warning; he just didn't come home from work one day. At first she thought he'd been mugged. Was lying somewhere in an alley, possibly bleeding out. She was so worried she called the cops. They wouldn't do anything, so she called his office. She got stonewalled—no information forthcoming. On the third day she drove over there herself and found a temp who walked her back to his cubby. Empty, the bulletin board just a bunch of colored pushpins and a ragged old *New Yorker* cartoon, one of those ones that made no fucking sense. Wasn't funny at all, that was a given, but also had no apparent meaning. Zero. Those cartoons, she'd always thought, were tests of something, and she failed the test. Who passed? She'd like to know. They put them in the magazine to enrage you. Smart people talking in code. Trying to bury you with their smartness. Like an autistic kid reeling off difficult calculations.

Had he actually liked it? Had he *gotten* it?

No way. There was nothing to get.

A gulf widened between them. She stared at the cartoon.

But maybe he'd just put it there for inspiration, for when he needed to be pissed off. Get a quick shot of adrenaline. For business purposes. Maybe the *New Yorker* cartoon was like a red flag to a bull.

Finally she asked someone, an older man she thought she recognized, although his name escaped her. All he said was, That guy? He quit. His assistant, Stacey, also quit. She had big bosoms. *Very* big. That was what the man said. "Big bosoms. *Very* big." Neither one of them gave any notice, he went on. We saw them drinking champagne at 11 a.m., then they were outta here.

When she got home she flipped out. She opened his file cabinet and found it almost completely empty. His birth certificate was gone, his Social Security card and tax files. In the bottom, a crumpled receipt for an oil change. That was it.

He wasn't using their joint credit card, she saw online; he'd always kept one of his own.

Big bosoms, she wrote in her journal. *Very big.*

Had Dan been a breast man? He never told her that. She was respectable. A 36C.

The men appeared a week later, when she was still on sick leave. Not actually sick, just crying, smoking and eating donuts. They offered to clean out the gutters, replace an AC filter and remove a dead limb from a tree; the limb, their spokesman said, was already splitting from the trunk. It could fall on her roof anytime. Cave it in. An injury could be sustained. Death might occur, even.

She was grateful; she hadn't noticed those things needed doing.

Lately she found she was getting so used to their support—logistical support, as she thought of it—that she began slacking off. *The men will do it*, she'd think, lying in bed, feeling the sun from the window slant across her face. *The men will handle it*. It used to be just the tasks that took muscle or mechanical know-how, but lately she'd even relied on them for housecleaning. Scrubbing, mopping, using a pumice stone on toilet rings.

She'd lie in her bed stretching out, lazing till late morning on the weekends, or put her feet up on a padded stool while resting in a large armchair, reading a novel about romance in a tropical setting. She'd watch a movie on demand and spoon ice cream straight from the carton, while in the shadows the men toothbrushed mold from the caulking between the shower tiles or ran vinegar through the dishwasher.

She didn't like the men to see her relaxing while they worked. She typically shut the bedroom door for privacy. Sometimes the spokesman needed to know something and knocked. Where did she keep the Shop-Vac? Did she own a Pozidriv screwdriver, or just that messy drawer of Phillips heads? Before she opened the door she'd pause the movie, turn off the monitor, hide the ice cream behind a potted plant, and spread out some paperwork on her bed. And when she opened the door she had to remind herself to squat, since the men took umbrage if you talked down to them.

As far as she could tell, they had a solemn respect for paperwork. "I better get back to my paperwork," she'd say, after a typically gruff exchange.

They cleaned with admirable thoroughness, though they tended to use way too much ammonia—enough to choke a horse. Once they polished a table so hard they stripped the stain right off the wood. Also, when they moved furniture to clean the floors, they always left it standing there in rectilinear formations. The men didn't know about asymmetry. Japan, feng shui, the men had no idea. Chairs sat opposite each other squarely, for instance, so that living-room guests would be forced to face each other down in staring contests. She had to go around sliding it back into place.

Homunculi, she wrote in her journal. *Defn: Diminutive human beings.* She never saw them outside the house—well, never past the boundaries of her property. In the backyard, sure, even out to the curb, which they sometimes skirted while mowing the lawn, but never at large on the street. They were her men, she guessed— at least partly. Possibly they came with the neighborhood association dues. Although when she was married she'd never seen them; back in those days they'd never come around. Maybe they figured that when you were married, you didn't need a team of men to help keep up. (They were wrong. In fact, when you were married you needed the men even more. When you were married you had to practically *beg* for help around the house.)

Technically she was still married, of course, but after all this time she had to figure that the men, like her, had realized Dan was never coming back. Dan was missing in action, where action was not some battlefield on foreign soil but their familiar life. Once familiar. Now faint. Sometimes Dan was an idea— Dan was a husband idea. The idea was draped over hangers in the closet. Drinking a cup of coffee at the counter. Reaching into the fridge for a beer. Dozing off in the middle of a pretty testy argument.

Sometimes he wasn't even an idea. Ideas could fade if you ignored them.

A bout of food poisoning laid her low after a burger-shack dinner with coworkers, and the next day, wretched, she caught sight of the men while she was dragging herself from her bedroom into the kitchen to pour a glass of water. They stood lined up outside her sliding doors, saluting from the patio. The salutes were jaunty: not exactly a joke, the men weren't inclined to humor, but there was a certain wit to the gesture. She padded across the rug in her socks and slid the doors open and then, instead of squatting — she was too weak for that, dehydrated from vomiting—sat down cross-legged on the floor, half-collapsed. She told them how sick she was, but they didn't need telling. They could see it, no doubt, from her sallow complexion and the greasy pants she'd slept in and hadn't bothered to change. In decent health she'd never show herself like this. Even to a dachshund.

The men suggested they fold her laundry, order some groceries for delivery. They said they could make dinner if she felt up to eating by evening, and if she didn't, no worries, it would keep. Maybe they'd even throw some entrées together for later in the week, lasagna or a ratatouille. Stick them in the freezer. They asked if she was counting carbs, or was it calories, and was she eating fish at the moment; they'd noticed she didn't buy poultry.

Their proposal seemed, at first, too personal. Was there a pair of underwear in the dryer, for instance? Well, she could always check . . . and cooking! They'd have to stand on stools to reach the stove. She could picture their stubby arms held over her gas burners as they reached toward the back for pots and pans—easy to set a sleeve on fire. The freezer, too, was out of reach. And yet they knew their own capacities; likely there wasn't any harm in it.

As she stood up, a wave of nausea making her sway and grimace, she thought maybe their spokesman had grown a bit. Of course that couldn't be. They were men, not boys, and had long ago reached puberty. She glanced at his feet: scuffed brown work boots. Probably in a little boys' size. Maybe they just had more of a heel on them than other shoes he wore.

Trial run, she thought. The men could cook for her this once. Her own cooking, if she was being totally honest—not so great. She mostly made pasta or salads. She'd tried a frittata last summer. Burned it.

It struck her, as it had several times before, to wonder what the men were getting out of this. At the beginning she'd assumed she'd be paying them, but they always waved off questions about how much she owed. If they didn't work for the neighborhood association, maybe their teamwork was some sort of government-subsidized employment program for the physically challenged—like the nearby community garden, staffed by three retarded guys, one of whom had grabbed her tits—but didn't want to ask in case it gave offense. She knew their height wasn't, to them, a disability as such. Only a characteristic. And it was true: it seemed to her, sometimes, like there was no domestic task the tiny men weren't equal to.

Still. Who would possibly wish to compensate the team for doing her cooking? Her laundry?

She'd have a frank conversation with the men as soon as she felt better. Very frank. Get to the bottom of their helpfulness.

She fell asleep for a long time after that and when she got up after twelve hours, ravenous, found her refrigerator and her freezer both well stocked. As usual they'd gone off without a word, but on her way out to the car she caught sight of the spokesman, pruning a jasmine vine on the side of the house. He was up on a stepladder.

She walked over, stood beneath him to thank him for all the meals. Sure, he was on a ladder, but this time she had to swear he was taller. And bulkier. You'd never see a dachshund this big. He was almost the size of a poodle. Standard.

"Listen, this is awkward," she said, squinting up. The sky was already bright. "It's—I just want to thank you for everything. Would you accept—compensation . . . ?"

The spokesman inclined his head a bit, acknowledging but not responding. Had he ever said more than five words to her in a row? It could be—she had to admit—frustrating, sometimes, the strong, silent position. Did you *have* to take the rough with the smooth? She waved and spun on her heel. Maybe the men were independently wealthy.

That afternoon she asked a couple of employees back to the house—make them feel comfortable with the boss. Outreach. Plus she could feed them the men's lasagna, have something homemade to offer. For once. A paralegal and an assistant. They came over bearing wine (the paralegal) and daffodils (the assistant) and though she didn't brag about the lasagna directly, she also didn't deny ownership. Hey. The men didn't ask for credit.

She drank most of the wine herself—the paralegal preferred beer and the assistant, a jack Mormon, was a total lightweight—and they laughed over the pieces of gossip the paralegal related. One of the lawyers had a serious foot fetish, according to his browsing history—not only a foot fetish but a fetish for dirty feet. A sales rep was having a steamy affair with the married head of HR. An IT guy, buddies with the paralegal, knew about it all.

Getting up from the couch around eleven, wondering when

they would leave, she tottered up the stairs to use the bathroom
and found two men beside her bed. For a moment she was taken
aback—it seemed intrusive. Oh, but they were doing a turn-down
service, that was all. One of them straightened as she came in,
leaving a foil-wrapped chocolate on her pillow. It looked comical,
him shimmying backward on his stomach off the side of the mat-
tress. He hadn't been able to reach her pillow without throwing
himself on top of the bed—but her bed was high, and, like the
spokesman, he seemed taller and broader-shouldered now than
he had before.

This was a first, she thought, the team performing tasks while
there were strangers in the house. (Plus, no one had asked them
for turn-down service. She'd never understood turn-down service. What was the point, for Chrissake?) She wished they'd come
downstairs and meet her coworkers. Maybe the paralegal or the
assistant would get the men to talk, for once.

But before she could invite them down—a nightcap? Just this
once?—they'd waddled past. They'd disappeared into Dan's man
cave, or what used to be. She followed, then saw she must have
been mistaken: they weren't there. She had to clean it out, put
his things in storage. Or should she just give them to Goodwill?
Yeah. Hell if Dan deserved storage. The dartboard, the photo of
his farmer grandparents that looked just like *American Gothic*,
even the high-school pole-vaulting trophy. She'd set it up as a
guest bedroom. Invite some guests.

In the living room the paralegal and the assistant had gotten
serious. They were talking in hushed voices when she came back
in, their heads close together.

"Oh. *Delia!*" said the paralegal loudly, interrupting what the
assistant was saying.

"That's my name," she said. "What, were you talking about me?"

"Ha *ha*!" said the paralegal.

"Oh my God," said the assistant. "It's so late! I had *no idea*! But wait. Which of us was the designated driver?"

After they left she thought about Dan. She'd thought it was a slump, but the slump had lasted a long time. Most days when they got home they hadn't even eaten together. He'd order pizza when she was trying to watch her weight, and then she'd make herself a salad. Or he'd come home with Chinese, enough for two but nothing that she liked. He'd eat the leftovers straight from the boxes the next night, not even heat them up. Cold and slimy. On weekend nights, he worked or he watched games; on Sunday he played golf, which was off limits to her. Once, not long before he left, he forgot his clubs but was still gone for six hours. He said he'd borrowed someone else's. "Testing a competition brand."

Occasionally they'd run an errand together, but even that had started to feel strained. When all you had was trips to Costco it wasn't a good sign.

What got to her was how he'd done it. That was what kept her up at night. Couldn't he have just said, like other guys did, hey, I want a divorce?

She'd never pegged him for a coward. He could be taciturn, he could be distant, but he wasn't guided by fear. He'd been in the army as a young man. Never saw combat, but still. No, it hadn't been fear and it hadn't been an oversight. "Shit! Almost forgot to tell you, honey, I'm leaving you tomorrow." He *wanted* to disappear. He *wanted* to leave her holding a bag of nothing.

Champagne at 11 a.m.

She wasn't even worth a goodbye.

In the morning she decided she'd call Goodwill. She needed

to eyeball the contents of the man cave quickly before she left to get a sense what size of truck they'd need. The door was closed—had she left it closed?—and when she pushed it open she gasped. Chair, desk, lamps, a rug, shelves. The metal file cabinet.

Nothing else.

All his personal effects were gone. Even the wall where the dartboard had been was bare, a field of dart-pricks around a clean circle.

Oddly what came to her first was *He's back.* Her heart raced.

But that ended. No one was back. Dan was in Fiji with very big bosoms. Or maybe Sacramento. (He always liked Sacramento. Another mystery.) The men had cleared it out, that was all. They'd taken care of it. She was confused, standing there in the doorway, about whether to be annoyed or grateful. How had they known?

She tried leaving money in an envelope for them on the table—five hundred bucks in cash, just a test since what they'd done was worth far more.

They didn't pick it up.

A few afternoons later she came home from work to find the front of her house barely visible beneath extensive scaffolding. The team was painting—six guys? No, all seven, painting the trim, the door, all the woodwork. She was attached to the colors of her house. It was fake Tudor, and the particular shades of brown and cream were based on some famous sixteenth-century building in England. She jumped out of her car and ran up the front walk.

"What's happening?" she called up. "What's going on?"

She looked—they were painting the rich brown a dull, flat gray—and started to panic a bit.

"But—" she called. "I like it the way it is!"

The spokesman, wearing paint-splattered overalls, looked down at her and nodded briefly. It seemed like a polite nod, but then he turned back to his work. Not listening to a word she said—the objection hadn't registered.

"Please! Guys! I really like the brown!" she repeated. The men went on painting.

She stood back and watched them for a while. Technically, if they wouldn't stop she could call the cops on them, but was she willing to risk their defection? Was she willing to give up everything they did? Eventually she sighed and shook her head and went in the side door. So they made a mistake every so often—well, rough with the smooth. Maybe the gray was a primer coat. Maybe they planned to freshen up the brown. It *had* been peeling here and there.

The sun was going down when they left for the day. She came out and looked up at the house. Still couldn't see much past the scaffolding, but enough to confirm the trim had in fact been changed from brown to gray. It wasn't a color she liked, but she could live with it, she guessed.

"Having some work done?" asked a neighbor man, pulling his garbage can to the curb. What was his name: Leon? Tony? Something like that.

"Yeah. Do you know those guys?" she asked.

They might have done some work for him—he wasn't married, for one thing. He might be eligible for their help. A confirmed bachelor. You could see why: a reddish wart on his cheek that looked like the bud of a dried-out rose. Spent most of his money on satellite dishes. They clustered on his roof. An NSA operative, maybe. Los Feliz branch.

"Technically, you need approval from the association," he said, squinting up at the scaffolding. "It's a historic district."

"But see, I never *asked* them to do it," she said. Defensive, sure—the guy was a busybody. "I didn't even *want* it changed."

"Yeah. Still. *Approval*," he said stiffly.

"Honestly," she said, "maybe you could get the homeowners' to speak to them? Maybe they'd make them paint it back. I feel like—it's out of my hands. Like I said. I didn't want it."

He looked at her, mouth agape. He shouldn't do that. It drew more attention to the wart. You saw the hole of the mouth, you saw the round wart so near, and you couldn't help thinking how the wart would fit right in the mouth.

Couldn't you get those things removed?

"Lost me. Your contractors aren't doing what you told them to?" he asked finally.

"I don't know if I'd call them contractors, per se," she said. "Maybe you've seen them around. The little men?"

He stared at her a minute longer, then shook his head.

"Been a goddamn long day," he said, and trudged back inside.

But then there was the removal of all her window treatments, leaving the light streaming in and no privacy from passersby on the street until she hung new ones. And then, because of her work schedule, she couldn't track them down to question them before they attached some vertical blinds she frankly couldn't stand— where were her plain white-cotton tab tops? Even their vintage hardware had disappeared, replaced by the cheap plastic doohickeys the vinyl strips were attached to. They switched out her multiple TV remotes for a "universal" one she didn't know to use; she couldn't even get the DVR to work.

She needed a sit-down with the men. Maybe it was the payment issue—maybe, though she'd offered, left the test envelope, her willingness to pay them hadn't been quite clear. Although, quite honestly, all these supplies: surely they wouldn't have gone out and bought them without approval, if they were strapped for cash?

At work, she went over to ask Cheryl, the paralegal, to notarize something but Cheryl wasn't at her carrel. On the screen the inbox was open, which normally wouldn't have caught her attention except that she saw her own face there. *Her* face was there in the body of the email, the headshot from her bio on the website, but it was attached to a cartoon body. She leaned closer to see.

It was some Disney thing—a still from the classic animated version of *Snow White*, was what it was. There was Snow White, in her yellow skirt and blue bodice, and beside her were seven dwarfs, their fat faces looking up at her with big, round noses, red like boozers'. The dwarfs were dipsomaniacs.

But Snow White had her own face, clumsily oversized for comic effect, Photoshopped on top of the cartoon body.

There was a caption underneath: *"But where's my Prince Charming?"* *"Sorry Snow White, he ran away with his secretary."*

She stood stock-still.

She must have mentioned the men, when they were drinking that night. Had she? She'd drunk too much of Cheryl's shitty wine. She must have let something slip.

She looked at the *From* line. The assistant.

Then at the recipients. There was a long list of them.

So fired. That assistant was gone.

"Oh." Now Cheryl was standing there. Triangulation. The image on the screen, Cheryl, and her.

"I'm sorry you had to see that," said Cheryl. Half-grimace, kind of trembling. Nervous. She should be. Guilt by association.

At *least*. Look at her face. Guilty as hell. Probably laughed her ass off.

"Why? It's hi*lar*ious," she told Cheryl. And smiled. As real as she could make it. "Love the Prince Charming line!"

She handed over the form. "Needs to be notarized," she said.

She walked away from Cheryl's carrel. A couple others glanced up from their desks as she passed—probably on the cc list. She smiled at them too. Like she was in on the joke. Always had been.

In her office she was agitated. Felt like high school again. Or middle school. Girls making fun of you behind your back. Huddled together. Their sidelong looks. Maybe you were wearing the wrong jeans. Maybe your zits weren't covered up. Or there was toilet paper on your shoe. Her face felt hot.

Brought up the assistant's personnel file. Eighteen egregious tardies in the past six months. Four screwups on shoots. It wouldn't be hard to justify. She'd wait, of course. Till more infractions were chalked up. It had to look justified.

Divorce was hard, people said. Yeah? Try desertion.

That night she found the kitchen half-gutted. They seemed to be remodeling it and had already retired for the night. Her stove was pulled out from the wall, refrigerator unplugged. Food had been neatly stored in coolers stacked against the wall—she was relieved it hadn't been left to rot—but it was hell finding what she'd wanted to eat for dinner beneath two pounds of cheddar, a tub of grapes and a milk jug.

Half the Marmoleum had been pulled up, too.

Obviously it couldn't stand. It had just gone too far.

She set her alarm for 5:30 so that the men, typically early risers, wouldn't have time to start before she woke up; she dressed and went down to the kitchen, made herself a cup of instant coffee in the microwave and planned what she would say. She had to be firm but polite—before this wrong turn they'd done so much for her—so she wrote a brief script for herself on her laptop in case she got nervous, drinking her coffee as she typed.

She was sitting in her living room with the mug in her hand and the laptop still open when the men came in. Through the front door, without knocking this time. (When was the last time they'd knocked?) But no. Impossible.

They were full-size.

She found she was speechless.

They filed by, seven of them; she counted as they headed down her hallway. Men of quite standard height—a mix of sizes, but all within the average range. The spokesman nodded at her and one or two made brief hand gestures too slight to interpret, but they passed by in no time, carrying tools and extension cords, businesslike. One of them struggled under the weight of a large box of ceramic tiles.

She felt rooted to her couch cushion.

She couldn't make the speech now, with the men so large. It was a shock. When they were small she'd had no trouble with any of it, but now . . . no. She couldn't tell them it was over, couldn't say she didn't want them to do any of this. Hadn't wanted a remodel. It wasn't—let's face it, it was like she didn't even own the place. It was like she wasn't even here.

She wasn't afraid—more like intimidated. She was reluctant, that was all she knew. She couldn't broach the subject.

Why should she, finally? She shouldn't *have* to.

But if she just went away she wouldn't have to deal with them; if she went away she could get a new place. She could finally sell this house. It was where she and Dan had lived. Another place, at least, would be her own. New start. There was a real-estate agent the paralegal had talked about: she could sell a house in no time, the paralegal said.

From the kitchen came the high whine of a drill.

She picked up her bag, slid the laptop in and went out the front door without looking back. Maybe a buyer would appreciate the kitchen remodel. She'd picked out the Marmoleum herself, back when she and Dan bought the place—well, maybe it wasn't for everyone. Same with the dull gray paint on the façade: a buyer might like the renovations, even if she didn't.

The men, now that she thought of it—possibly they were helping. Facilitating her transition. Maybe somehow they'd known the best course. She'd needed a nudge to help her move on, hadn't she? Too long in this house, too long in limbo. Dan was gone, but she lingered. She was the ghost, not him.

No doubt at all: they were intuitive. They had instincts. At the beginning, at least, they'd closely anticipated so many of her needs . . . lately they'd taken too much initiative, true. Lately they'd seemed to veer off course. But now she was thinking it hadn't been a wrong turn after all. Maybe the men knew what they were doing.

She knew she was coming back tonight—of course she was, she had to pick up some clothes—but it felt like she was running away. Sometimes running away was the best. The best! Beneath her feet was cool, cool grass.

The neighbor man who'd reprimanded her was getting in his car, no briefcase but a suit. Leon/Tony. She caught his eye and waved at him as she ran—no wave back, of course—before she realized she'd passed her own car and had no clear destination. Only then did she also realize she'd left her ring of keys on the table in the front hall. What was the plan, anyway?

She ground to a halt lamely and watched the neighbor's car pull out, drive to the corner and turn.

She'd get a hotel room for tonight, then find a short-term

rental. That was all. Not rocket science. She'd built her own company, for Chrissake. She could do it.

She looked back at her front door. It seemed darker and heavier now, almost to pulsate. Maybe the men had sensed that she was making her escape. Maybe it angered them.

Still, she needed the car key. But wait: she used to keep the spare in her laptop bag. Was it still there?

She rummaged.

No.

So she went to the door, opened it quietly. She could hear them in the kitchen, sawing or drilling. She saw the keys splayed on the hall table, with her sunglasses. Approached stealthily, grabbed them both.

As she turned to go, she caught sight of the spokesman in the living room. He sat on her couch, exactly where she'd been sitting. The leather was probably still warm from her ass. The TV was on—some morning show. He held the universal remote in one hand, and with the other hand was eating a burrito. Cramming it into his mouth like he was ravenous. The wrapper lay unfolded on the couch arm beside him.

He swiveled his head toward her. That was how it seemed: he was an ancient beast, a beast of prey. He'd spotted his quarry, and his head swung round to fix on it. He chewed.

Then he swallowed. And nodded.

"Hey," he said.

His voice was low.

Her arm was trembling, so she raised the hand with the keys. Did she smile, or was it a grimace? She jangled the keys in a kind of hasty response.

And fled.

FIGHT NO MORE

The mornings had been bitter in recent weeks. They had a faint, chemical bitterness, he couldn't say whether it was taste or smell. Like the lemons that grew on those public trees they watered with sewage. He'd seen them in desert cities on tour— Tucson, maybe Phoenix. They looked like lemons, but they weren't for eating. Could the birds tell? Don't peck *those* lemons, friend. But maybe birds didn't like lemons anyway. Or maybe some birds were shit-eating birds.

He'd woken up into that bitterness every morning, at once vague and sharp. This was its culmination, like he'd known of the coming death and his mood had been soured by the foreknowledge. Come autumn maybe he'd get free of the city for a weekend, drive up into the trees in the Sierras—maybe that would do it. Or down into the oak scrublands in the hill country east of San Diego. He'd go there to mourn, and a chill would sweep in and clean out the ill taint.

He didn't know anyone at the service well. Lordy hadn't come, no surprise. Probably sitting at home in an unlit room, singing. That was Lordy's ritual when he was threatened by chaos of mind: he'd sit singing into the dimness for hours on end. Ry'd heard the dark singing one time and it sounded high and eerie as a boy soprano—a warbling falsetto sung by a baritone, the keening of a hurt beast. After he sang himself out, his voice was rough and scratchy for days. You'd suspect he was deeply disturbed unless you knew him, in which case you were *sure* he was deeply disturbed. But you also reckoned there were coping strategies behind it. Lordy was a lunatic who came bearing gifts. High-functioning.

When you brought that level of value, a label executive had said of Lordy's music, there *was* no sane and no insane. There was nothing but product.

That was the story of the market, the guy from the label had bloviated. And the story of the market was *the greatest story ever told*.

He'd pronounced that sanctimonious shit and all Ry could think of was how he himself was only a neurotic, he had a minor-league anxiety compared to Lordy's full-fledged bipolarity and a minor-league talent to go with it. For genius, either ruthlessness or real insanity was needed. It was both a stupid myth and a stupid truth. The sane, in the end, were only the workhorses of music.

It saddened him to contemplate his relative mental stability. Not a damn thing he could do about it, either.

Distraction. He didn't want to be here. From his seat at the end of the pew he scanned other pews for a familiar face, but the rows were dark-clothed bodies and goose-fleshed skin in the artificial chill, the faces pale half-moons. Most of the crowd was young, Lynn's students from the high school—clearly he'd been popular. He'd kept teaching even once they started recording, took his sick days when he was needed in the studio.

No one knew Ry and he knew no one. No one he could see, anyway. Only the solidity of grief saved him from panic at being hemmed in—at any other time, when he wasn't weighed down, the crowds would have been his cue for a fast exit. Onstage and in the studio he'd learned to deal, but outside those spaces, with people around and no instrument to shield him, it wasn't always clear where he should put his body. He often felt extra, unneeded in a scene. He had no lines. He had no role. How did you hold yourself so as to not feel spare?

He kept getting mental pictures of the accident, though he hadn't seen it. The cops said a jacked-up truck had clipped the Fat Boy, passing illegally on the right and crossing into the lane at 90 or 95, and bumped it into the air—a bump he couldn't stop his brain from trying to frame. The bike crashed into a concrete barrier, they said. Lynn's neck had snapped.

He'd been on his way to a session so they'd been waiting for him when it happened. He didn't show up and didn't show up, and didn't answer any calls or texts, and it was so out of character that finally Ry drove Lordy to his house and used the key he kept under an empty plant pot to get in. They'd only been there a couple of minutes when the cops came to the door, two cops, a young one who talked and an older one who stood behind him. Lordy'd nodded slowly during their rigid announcement—the young policeman had delivered the news nervously, like maybe he'd never done that duty before. But after the cops left he started shaking so rapidly and mechanically it looked like some kind of seizure. Ry'd just stood there repeating: "Why did he take the freeway? Why did he take the freeway? He always took surface streets. Why did he take the freeway?"

After a bit Lordy had stopped shaking and left. He'd stumbled out of the house while Ry was in shock, just wandering around the rooms thinking *Lynn won't be here again.*

No word since.

He blinked, lashes wet feathers on his cheeks. Wiped the back of his sleeve over them. Up at the front some guy was talking, a mass of words, forgotten almost as soon as they were said.

Ry'd always liked words but they were flat without music. Dry.

The Fat Boy never had loud pipes. It ran quiet, not obnoxious Lynn's father had rebuilt it with his own hands, before he lost the use of them. Parkinson's. Lynn was attached to it for that reason. And for *the feel of movement,* he'd told Ry and Lordy, *not just through space but time.* Lynn was about rhythm, not speed—had never sped when he rode. Never sped when he drummed, either. Everything at the right tempo.

The driver of the jacked-up truck just kept going. Kept right on moving down the 10. Never looked back. All the way to the Mojave Desert, likely. Over the Colorado into Arizona, New Mexico, Texas. The Eastern Seaboard. Who knew. They had a partial plate from a witness: two digits, California. That was it.

Unfair. Unfair. Fucking unfair. But to cling to it was so useless it was borderline stupid. *Unfair* was what kids whined when they didn't get what they wanted. When they made that complaint— his six-year-old niece said it constantly—you told them some lazy shit like, *Well, life isn't always fair.* Lazy shit sure, but true as dirt. You also taught them to believe it *should* be fair, so they could grow up and be confused forever by the tension between what was and what should be. He wasn't a father, small mercies. Hoped never to be. He'd seen firsthand how raw it made you. Might as well strip your clothes off and run naked down High Street in a hail of gunfire.

That was being a parent.

The truck driver kept on driving. People who drove too fast for the hell of it were the worst kind of bastards, the kind who believed the world belonged to them.

And they were right. It did.

Someone wept raggedly in the front pew—one of Lynn's sisters, he thought, peering over while trying to seem like he wasn't. She began to hyperventilate, or that was how it looked to him— trouble breathing, shaking her head—and was led out through a door near the altar. Was the girlfriend here? Nina? She must be, lost in the gathering. From the outside Nina and Lynn had seemed like an odd couple, since he was a six-foot-five black man and she was a five-foot-four white woman, but soon after they met they'd been together whenever they could.

He'd only been to services for old people before, solemn but still within the natural order—his grandfather, grandmother, a great-aunt. Oh, except for one: when he was a junior in high school, soon after the move from Brisbane to L.A., a senior had died in the middle of a baseball game. Hit hard in the chest by a ball and fell down dead—a massive coronary. Ry remembered thinking: Is this what happens in America? Back in Australia, no kid in his small world had died. The senior's parents said he'd had a heart condition since birth. "He always knew it was a risk. He wanted to play the sports he enjoyed." The whole school had attended the memorial, standing room only. The dead boy, though a sporty type, had also been a fan of *The Rocky Horror Picture Show*. They all were back then—at least, most of the kids he knew. It was back in the early eighties, when fans dressed up and went to the midnight shows. He remembered clearly because at the memorial they played the theme song, "Science Fiction, Double Feature."

Back then they went to watch a film about transvestite aliens, humanoid scientists in drag who made beautiful Frankenstein monsters in silver Speedos and ate the body of Meatloaf out of a coffin. They dressed in drag and wore towering black wigs with white stripes in them; they sang along to songs about unbridled lust and the joys of heroin. Later they turned into claims adjusters and bank tellers, gas station attendants and divorce lawyers.

He hadn't known the dead boy. Everyone went so he went—it would be more remarkable to avoid the service than attend it—but once there he felt like an impostor.

But how much better to feel that way than this.

Now he hung back as they all filed out. He stayed sitting for so long that everyone had to leave from the other end of the pew. He couldn't mobilize. The crowds disappeared through the tall double doors at the back and he was left alone with the portrait at the front. Got up finally and walked over.

Closed casket; the photograph on its brass stand was all there was to see. And the picture was formal, Lynn posed in a jacket and tie. It looked like Lynn had posed for a shot he didn't have much interest in. But you could still make out the modesty of the smile, its humility.

The address for the reception was on his phone. Near Lynn's place at Lordy's uncle's house, though Lordy was almost certain to be absent. Ry hadn't wanted to drive, had called up an Uber—now another, and he didn't register much as they floated along. The streets were a scene from other people's lives. Today more than most days. Ugly city, except where the rich lived. Los Angeles was stark like that. Ugly where money wasn't, beautiful where it was. Well, not always. Along the beach even the rich lived in ugly buildings.

You did what you knew how to do. Was there anything else?

He'd been here a couple of times before, once for a quinceañera, once for a Super Bowl party, both times as Lordy's chaperone. And driver: Lordy was afraid of driving, had an actual phobia and no license, so he'd bought the biggest and thickest-walled car on the market and made Ry or sometimes Lynn drive it. Ry had a stipend from Lordy to be his chauffeur. Lordy's idea, but he'd said yes. Gratefully. Bass player/chauffeur, his job description. Sometimes he feared the chauffeur job was his real one. Shit, he had more income from it. Far more.

The house wasn't big, just a ranch-style on a working-class street, but the backyard was surprisingly vast, green as a jungle, and that was where the fiestas were held. There were avocado trees, grapefruit, magnolia, all with delicate lights strung through them; there was one of those concrete triple-decker fountains that looked like a cake stand in a bakery. Moving beneath the trees, he flicked his eyes around for someone to give his condolences to: once that was done, he would be free. He could go.

He knew the sister, and the brother who'd been in jail, but he didn't see either of them yet. Lynn's parents were long gone.

But wait: Nina. She stood in a corner of the yard under a trellis with some white-flowered vine, a small, beaded purse over one shoulder and a glass held out in front of her. It was connected to her but also separate, less drink than personal shield. Her face was void, like someone had poured it out. She was a realtor; Lynn had met her while they were shopping for a house for Lordy. It had been a disaster, since Lordy decided, out of sight of any of them, to plunge into the house's deep lap pool. They found him just in time. Lynn had to give him CPR.

No idea what to say, but he got his own drink from a table. Then he was walking along a pebbled path to where she stood staring, absentminded.

"Nina."

"Oh. Ry."

They stiffly embraced, separated, then stood there with their drinks. Sipping, maybe, more often than they strictly needed to. He wasn't sure whether he should offer condolences—the loss was both of theirs. Were you supposed to measure the losses against each other, give condolences according to whose loss was greatest? He'd known Lynn for longer, and worked with him and spent more time, but she was the girlfriend. Position of privilege. Always implicit: friendship was secondary. The world of couples was one that you were in or out of, and he was out. Always had been.

Even when he was seeing someone, a rare event, he never entered that enclosed world. Couples established themselves with lines you couldn't cross. They were each other's barricades.

She and Lynn, though, had been good company together. No private jokes to show how intimate they were. Attentive to the third wheel, both of them. She was tough in some ways, at times a little paranoid, but smart. And devoted to Lynn. He would've liked her for that devotion alone.

But she was crying now, her nose and eye makeup running, so he took her arm and led her to a stone bench under a tree. They faced away from everyone—people were beginning to trickle in, emerge slowly through the back door, speaking in low voices. She fished around in her bag. Tissue. Off to their right the fountain made its sound, but it wasn't like nature or streams. It made him think something was leaking. Somewhere a pipe had broken under the surface, and slowly, unseen, dark waters were rising.

"Sorry. I thought I'd keep it together in public," she said, shaking her head. "Sorry. Embarrassing."

It was easier to be with someone who didn't expect him to act at ease, less lonely to stand beside someone sunk into their own well. His well wasn't far off, and from the bottom of one you couldn't see into the other, but at least you knew it was there.

Usually after ten minutes he would have slipped away to a private space, a bathroom or bedroom. In such places his custom was to look at himself steadily in whatever mirror he could find. It calmed him down to see his reflection, because it could be anyone's. You're not so different, you're just a guy—a quiet guy who plays bass. They can't see through your skin to the alarm you feel when their eyes rest on you. *See? Fear is invisible.*

"I had a win," she said, when she finished dabbing at her face. She was mumbling.

"Uh. Pardon?"

"I had a way in."

Still he could barely hear her.

"A way into the world. For the first time. He was my only way in."

He wasn't sure what she meant. This gray area, this stretching grayness that was the unspeakable quality of feeling, could only be captured by rhythm and melody.

"People say, you know, time will help heal it," she went on. "It won't be so acute. That could be true. It has to be. No one can live like this."

She was in her well and thought she'd never get out. And he had to admit, it was distinctly possible. A nurturing-type person would probably cluck like a chook and reassure her, but he didn't have that in him. He could barely say regular things.

He'd rather tell her the truth, anyway: a well was deep and true and had its own cylindrical perfection. It gave good shelter because its walls weren't thin; they were as thick as the earth was round. When you were in a well the walls went on forever.

From the solitude of a well, if you were fortunate, you could look up now and then and see a circle of sky. That circle might as well be the world, or the span of a life in it—clouds passed in the blink of an eye, no matter how immense they were. Stars greater than the sun shone down, as small as pins, from infinite remove.

Course, you couldn't say hard things, not when times were already hard. He knew that much. Only music could cross the divide. The brain's hard wiring, probably, how music resonated—said everything while saying nothing at all. But he preferred to think of it in less scientific terms. Music, the hard currency of the soul.

"I should go talk to his family," she said. "He made me his executor. We were going to—we hadn't told anyone yet, but we had agreed to get married."

"Oh," he said. He almost added *Congratulations*. Stopped himself. Lynn hadn't mentioned it, but it made sense.

"It wasn't going to be a big thing, just a small ceremony," she said. "But he wanted to be organized. He had a will. I don't. I don't own much, so what's the point."

"He had the house," said Ry, nodding. His father had left it to him. House, bike and gold record.

"He wants—wanted the house to go to his siblings," she said. "To sell. I guess none of them wants to live in it. I'll be—it's going to be my job to sell it for them."

"You don't have to," he offered. "It might be easier—someone who's not—"

"I know. But I want to. To look out for them. You know? They don't know much about real estate."

The phrase *real estate* made the conversation everyday. They were two people talking about real estate.

She felt it too, he thought. Almost ashamed. Or maybe he was reading too much into it. She dabbed at her eyes with the tissue.

"OK," she said. "I'll go. Do I look—?"

"Fine," he said, though there were still faint eye-makeup tracks.

She smiled at him, small smile. Reached out and squeezed his hand. Then walked away, purse over one shoulder, holding the drink.

Missed Connections, he thought. It was a section in Craigslist. People who saw each other on the bus. Or at a restaurant. As far as he could tell all connections were missed.

Or all his, anyway. He'd read an email recently, he shouldn't have but it was over his sister's shoulder, half by accident while he was helping her troubleshoot on her computer. She was divorced and dating some guy—she constantly had to hire babysitters so she could go out with him. When she ran low on cash Ry was the babysitter. All Ry knew about him was that when they first met he liked her for her English accent. She had to break it to him that the accent was Australian. She said he seemed kind of disappointed.

The email was from the guy. "Thanks for the hours of deep connection," it said. Did that ring true to her?

It didn't ring true to him.

Was it enough to *think* you had a "deep connection"?

Maybe it was. Maybe that was all that counted, in the end. Maybe illusion was everything.

Unexpected sight at the back door: a fake leopard-skin hat. Beneath it, Lordy, facing the floor. He rarely looked up, in public. Now he was shuffling along in a black suit and shoes Ry had never seen before—glossy loafers. Tassels. He usually wore tailored shoes in some vegan fabric, slip-ons. No laces. He didn't like laces; he claimed he couldn't tie a bow. He never learned, he said. These couldn't be leather—impossible. Even in his expensive SUV, whose high-end package came with all-leather upholstery, he had insisted on vinyl seats. The day they'd picked up the car from the dealership, after a long wait, it turned out the steering wheel had leather trim on it.

But since Lordy would never touch the wheel himself they'd been able to conceal it from him. Lynn went so far as to complain about the texture of the grip, grumbling to Lordy that when his hands sweated the vinyl was slippery beneath them.

When it came to Lordy, Ry was sometimes unsure how to proceed but Lynn had been confident. Lynn hadn't been above a white lie.

Now the job of white lies would be all on him.

So vinyl loafers. And who had driven him? Maybe he'd walked. He liked to walk, and because he didn't drive he often walked for miles.

Ry approached quickly, from the side. Best not to pop up suddenly in front of Lordy: it could make him jump.

"There's lemonade, if you're thirsty," he said. Lordy didn't touch spirits. That was how he put it, when they were offered to him. "I never touch spirits," he'd mumble.

"Lemonade," repeated Lordy, but at the same time shook his head. His eyes darted. That meant he had no interest in a drink. With Lordy you had to read the signs, not listen to the words.

Behind him a young kid Ry'd never seen before struggled to push a cart with equipment on it, an amp and keyboard and loops of cable.

"What's this?" said Ry.

"Chair!" said Lordy gruffly, so Ry turned and went through the back door. At the kitchen table all the chairs were taken, but Lynn's sister was carrying platters into the dining room and as she passed he asked if they could spare one. She tapped another woman on the shoulder, and slowly the woman stood. Ry thanked her as he picked up the chair—rickety, but it would have to serve.

Outside Lordy was watching as the kid ran the cable to an outlet on the house's back wall. He saw Ry and the chair and pointed with an impatient hand to an area beside the triple-tiered fountain, a piece of pavement beneath a mimosa tree.

"There," he muttered, still facing the ground.

He sat on the chair, plugged the keyboard into the speaker and played a couple of chords, testing. The sound carried well. No eye contact. He didn't wait for an audience, either.

"Traditional version," he said. Ry doubted anyone else heard. "English."

Then he started playing. Even on one keyboard, it sounded like an orchestra. His voice was deep and full.

"Arise, ye workers from your slumber / Arise, ye prisoners of want," he began.

More guests were filing out the back door, their conversations subsiding. Nina was among them; her hand trembled holding her glass. It was empty anyway so he took it from her and held it himself.

"No more deluded by reaction / On tyrants only we'll make war / The soldiers too will take strike action / They'll break ranks and fight no more," sang Lordy.

Around them the crowds were so thick pushing out of the house, almost jostling, that Ry stumbled forward.

"It's Lordy," whispered a teenage girl.

"And the last fight let us face!" shouted Lynn's brother, the jailbird. He had no singing voice at all.

More of them sang, not shy but lagging, since only the family really knew the words. Lynn had played recordings of the song at family gatherings, and other than the brother they all had good ears.

This wasn't the kind of thing Lordy usually did. He'd always dismissed the song. "Commie propaganda," he'd once said to Lynn when Lynn was picking it out on a guitar, though he'd been smiling his lopsided grin when he said it. "White-people shit." You could never tell what that grin meant: sometimes it was intended gently, fondly; other times it was almost malicious.

And the setting was way outside Lordy's usual comfort zone. As he sang, and the mourners went along, game for the tribute but pretty much butchering the lyrics, Ry wondered if he'd have to shepherd Lordy out afterward. Lordy was at his best before a performance and at his worst afterward, the exact opposite of Ry, who felt satisfied after he played, a task complete. But Lordy was filled with emotion and often shaky or explosive. Angry at small mistakes, mostly other people's but sometimes his own—mistakes no one else ever noticed.

When he finished a silence fell. And held. The song had got to them. Lordy was magic.

He made you pay to be near him, though. You paid for the alchemy. No gold without a pound of flesh.

The silence went on until Lynn's brother shouted "Encore!"

No surer way to piss Lordy off.

But he didn't pitch a fit. Relief. He just got up and walked back toward the house through the crowd. It parted like the Red Sea.

Lordy had a strong sense of what he needed to do at any given time. Only at the swimming pool had he hesitated. He lacked some basic skills: tying shoelaces, driving, swimming. He'd never learned even a basic front crawl, but that day, he told Ry later, he just really wanted to swim. The blue water had called to him.

"I'm off," Ry told Nina, and handed her back the empty wineglass.

And he did what he always did: followed the leader.

I KNEW YOU IN THIS DARK

After the service, for the first time since high school, she'd learned part of a poem by heart. It was a World War I poem, written for the dead. *They shall not grow old, as we that are left grow old. / Age shall not weary them.* She wasn't sure how the minister had chosen it. Lynn wasn't English or a soldier.

But like a soldier he'd died young.

She dropped the words she didn't like from the poem and kept the rest. Ran over it in her head when she felt the fast clutch of grief. *To the innermost heart . . . they are known / As stars are known to the night.*

She often listened to the music he'd played for her after dinner, drink in hand. She'd doled out most of his collection to the guys in the band, including his hundreds of carefully kept records. It hadn't been easy to split them up, but the others treasured them: she could tell by the way they handled the grainy cardboard of the covers. For herself she'd reserved only the music he'd played for her when they were together, on his MP3 player and a small shelf of CDs. She kept these beneath a picture of him she'd taken with her phone and printed out at the office, and a votive candle she lit at night.

Bereavement had made her into an audience at work. The clients talked to her more than they had before, not casual conversations but confessions. Some new receptiveness must be coming off her, a helpless openness she didn't want.

She'd had some doozies lately, client-wise. A magnet for eccentrics. There was a man who told her all about his shameless infidelity as though the telling would absolve him. A buyer from Redondo Beach showed her graphic pictures on his phone of a recent liposuction procedure; someone from out of state, calling to list her boyfriend's condo, told all about his criminal conviction. There was a seller in Los Feliz who confided that her house was infested with handyman midgets. She was a successful executive at a production company—mostly local and regional commercials—and appeared to lead an otherwise normal life. But she'd had to leave her house, she told Nina, when the midgets grew into regular-sized men overnight. "*Seven* of them," she told Nina, indignant. "There wasn't room for all of us."

This house—an overpriced wreck near the Hollywood sign— was owned by a woman who claimed to be a vampire and said she could only draw strength from drinking blood.

"I used to be a med sang," she said, "you know, a medical san- guinarian? But then I got into the lifestyle." She'd had a boyfriend who let her feed on him, but after that ended—for unrelated reasons, she clarified—she'd gotten used to buying blood online. She kept it lined up in small jars, vacuum-sealed and neatly labeled with the dates of purchase, in her refrigerator, where dark liver and fillets of deep-pink salmon also glistened under Saran Wrap. The freezer was fitted with an actual padlock. They didn't discuss it.

The vampire house was decorated with paintings of thin, beautiful Goths pierced by knives, their skin white, hair dark, lips red. Snakes twined around them as they lay, or if they stood, fierce wolves crouched at their feet, showing oversized fangs. Crows spread black wings on bare shoulders.

Lynn's sister's kids liked vampire shows. Well, the girl liked vampires but the boy said vampires were lame, zombies better. But there weren't good zombie shows for kids, so he streamed episodes of *The Walking Dead* on his iPad on the sly. But he wasn't sly enough and got in trouble. Lynn's sister said the zombie-butchering wasn't healthy. She said it would give him nightmares, then make him want to stockpile guns or take up the crossbow. He said, "What, I'm gonna wake up one day and start hacking off people's rotting limbs?" The little girl, who was only eleven, avidly watched the *Twilight* franchise. She was allowed because her mother watched with her and thought the actors and actresses were cute. She dreamed of becoming the undead. That was true love to her: in true love you found an undead boyfriend and, admittedly after some back-and-forth, agreed to be undead for him.

The little girl had asked: "If Uncle Lynn came back from the dead and said he was a vampire now, would you let him bite you?" Yes, Nina had admitted. "Yes, I believe I would." Bite me. The cold skin wouldn't be great at first, but she could get used to it.

The vampire didn't want to show her house without its human-skull candles and refrigerated blood supply. She said at first, with confidence, that another vampire would probably make an offer. Nina had warned her that the vampire community might not be large enough to meet the asking, but the homeowner was stubborn. She said the MSM—which referred to "mainstream media," according to Siri—had *no idea* how large the vampire community was. There was a conspiracy afoot to deny its size and power, for the vampire lobby boasted rock stars and captains of industry. Some, the homeowner strongly implied, were household names. They didn't come out of the closet because of (a) their careers and (b) the fact that it was a secret society.

Nina had said, "I understand, but is there a large vampire *real-estate*-buying community?"

The vampire said she'd put the word out, but so far no vampire buyers had stepped up.

Without a concept of the future all sense of urgency disappeared. No momentum. That was why she seemed like a patient listener to the clients: she had nowhere better to be. Before Lynn, it was true, she'd had only the vaguest sense of her future, but then the future had arrived. Now it was past.

How to honor his memory? That was a question the grief counselor had suggested. Sometimes the woman used words that reminded her of Marnie, expressions her sister relied on such as *get clarity* and *self-actualize*. "Do you consider yourself self-actualized?" the counselor had asked. "I don't know what it means, so I guess no," she'd said.

They'd had a meeting with an insurance salesman lined up. Lynn had wanted them to have life-insurance policies—mainly him, so that she'd be "taken care of." She'd thought it was old-mannish and smiled when she said yes. But then he died. What she had now was her job. Technically, it was all she had. That, a rented house and a leased Mercedes SUV she spent hours in every day and didn't even like. A gas-guzzler.

Lynn had loved her the way she was, he always claimed, but without him she wasn't even the way she *had* been. He wouldn't love her how she was now. Staying in at night and watching bad reality shows. She watched a show about people who had romances with inanimate objects: one woman claimed to be involved with a carnival ride. It was a semi with the ride attached on a crane-like mechanism, and the woman had candlelight dinners inside the truck. She set a place for the ride, a plate with food on it and a goblet. There was also a man who introduced his father to his red sports car; the car was his fiancée, he said. The father was visibly uncomfortable. The man kissed his car on camera, proclaiming his engagement, then using his tongue. He also "made love" to it, as the narrator said, but that part was pixelated.

At the office they claimed the show was faked, but she wasn't so sure.

Another show featured people who consumed non-food items. One woman ate the stuffing out of her furniture. Whole mattresses and couches disappeared. Another snorted talcum powder, bowls and bowls of it every week. Been doing it for years, the narrator said. Her living room was covered in a dusting of white like new-fallen snow. They took her to the doctor to show her how unhealthy the habit was, but her lung scans came up clear. The doctor couldn't believe it. The furniture-eater was unimpressed. It was understandable—her lungs were pink as a baby's. She'd go on huffing the powder, she said, in that case. Why not?

Lynn would not be proud of how she spent her evenings. And

yet—it was a blanket. It was a dull roar. He didn't know how much she missed him, how sharp the hurt but thin and dull the knives.

If he knew, she told herself, he'd forgive her.

This would be her eighth showing of the vampire house; the homeowner was absent, thankfully, off at her job in the Valley, which seemed to be either in phone sales or sex work, unclear which. Maybe both. How she'd afforded the house in the first place was also unclear. Twice she'd insisted on being present at showings, always a bad idea but very bad when the seller was a vampire. The first time, she opened the door to Nina and the clients in a black-latex bodysuit. She didn't say much—that was a plus—but the prospective buyers, two men from Encino with blond brush cuts, spent the whole tour looking at her cleavage, or alternately at her ass. It was a joke from the get-go.

The second time, after Nina requested—at least—please, less distracting clothes, she wore a white robe and dangling earrings with ankhs the size of lollipops. The robe was harmless, but then there were the fingernails—red, three inches long, and curved. That time the potential buyers were an elderly, retired couple. The wife kept looking at the talons nervously.

These prospective buyers were hoping to flip it: you couldn't beat the location. They said they had Chinese investors, which the VOF supported. But they were late. She'd give it fifteen more minutes, then call or text. She had to be at another house by two.

The kitchen was in minor disarray—a puddle of coffee on the counter, a bowl in the sink. She wiped the counters down, washed the bowl and put it away, stuck some forks and knives into the dishwasher. She took a wadded dishrag into the laundry room, threw it into the hamper, and went back into the kitchen to inspect her handiwork. Presentable, though not sparkling.

Opening the fridge to make sure it was tidy as well—she typically shoved the blood jars behind a carton of OJ; apparently vampires needed vitamin C—she saw the padlock on the freezer above it was dangling open. Reflexively she put her hand up to click it closed, but as her fingers touched the cold metal she stopped.

Slowly she moved her hand to the edge of the door. Slowly, looking over her shoulder once, almost superstitiously, she pulled it open.

A gallon carton of ice cream, Rocky Road. Behind it, mounds of Ziploc bags. Brown inside. She reached for one, pulled it out. It had a date in red marker. What, a wig? She turned it over in her hands. A furry head. A face. Closed eyes.

It was a squirrel.

She practically threw it back in. As she pushed to find a place for it on the heap, other, smaller bags fell forward, slipping over each other onto the plastic edge. She grabbed at them to stop the collapse. A flattened rat; she saw the tail. Several white mice stuffed into a single bag, their minuscule pink feet. Behind the cascade, something larger. She didn't have to touch it to see what it was: a tabby cat. Orange stripes. Horrible mouth, pulled rigidly open.

The doorbell rang, its chime the deep toll of a church bell.

She stuffed them back in and clicked the padlock.

At least it hadn't been severed human limbs, she told herself as she went to open the door. Could have been worse. The cat, though. Could you order *them* online? Maybe you could, for science class or something. Dissection lessons.

The prospects were impatient, although they were the ones who'd been late. They took the tour, but mainly were inter-

ested in the house's footprint. They held blueprints and walked
around pointing at walls, talking rapid-fire in what she assumed
was Mandarin. Although it might have been Cantonese. Lynn
had taught her the difference, that one was spoken in mainland
China, the other in places like Taiwan. The Chinese liked Lordy's
music. The prospects barely noticed the décor. Couldn't have
cared less about the knife-pierced Goths or stuffed bats in the
corners of ceilings—bats she'd thought might be alive the first
time she saw them. They hung from the ceiling beams the way she
thought living bats might hang and were very large—flying foxes,
the vampire said, shipped from Australia. She'd tried keeping live
bats, she told Nina, but it turned out they were disease vectors.
Plus the guano. They'd shitted everywhere. And then they died.
Maybe she wasn't giving them the right food, maybe she'd got
the diet wrong. Some bats ate insects, said the vampire. Others
preferred ripe fruit.

When the potential buyers finally left—no decision yet—
she had to race to get to her next appointment. It was the house
belonging to the woman who imagined midgets; the woman met
her in the front yard, saying she didn't go inside herself anymore.
The house had been emptied by the moving company.

"I realize they're probably not in there right at the moment,"
the woman told her. "But it would just be so awkward if I saw
them again. You know?"

"OK," said Nina. She'd never seen anyone in the house but two
painters she'd hired on the seller's behalf. And the cleaners.

They had some papers to sign, which they accomplished on the
hood of Nina's car. Then the woman drove off, leaving Nina to
meet with an inspector and later an AC repair guy.

There was a hatch to the attic, and Nina followed the inspec-

tor up the drop-down ladder, mostly for the hell of it. The roof hung low over them; she could stand upright but the inspector had to stoop a bit. The attic hadn't been cleaned out. A plaid blanket was spread in the middle of the floor, with some bedrolls neatly rolled up at one end of it. Coolers were stacked on the other side.

"Like someone had a little picnic here," said the inspector. "I'll tell you what, though: the sub-roof needs replacing. This thing's forty years old if it's a day. You see how the OSB is warped? That piece right there looks like a boomerang. You tore it off and threw it, it'd probably come right back to you."

She nodded as he ticked a box on his handheld device. The woman who saw midgets was in a hurry to sell and wouldn't bat an eyelash at the markdowns.

Driving home she took surface streets, as she almost always did since Lynn died on the 10. Tomorrow would be tough. First thing in the morning she had to meet his sister and brother at the house, help them to divvy up the last few sticks of furniture. The only bone of contention so far had been their father's gold record from his Motown days; they both wanted that. In the end they played rock-paper-scissors. Best of three. The brother won.

She'd shown Lynn's house with most of the furniture still in it, and it had sold surprisingly fast. Multiple bidders. She didn't know enough about the neighborhood to know how typical that was, but she'd never been so relieved to sell a property. Walking through the rooms, listening to clients dismiss the place offhand, disparage its contents—it wasn't the only time she'd hated her job, but it was the worst. After the second showing she'd acquired the habit of popping a Valium before she went in and telling them right off that the house had been in her family until a sudden

recent death. That shut them up, more or less. Luckily it didn't stop them from bidding.

After that she had to go to a hotel in Playa del Rey. The first day of a self-help seminar her sister wanted her to do. She wasn't looking forward to it, but she would endure it and after she endured, she would call Marnie. She'd know what to say, armed with the right jargon. Marnie had made it a condition: if they were to be close again, she had to do the seminar.

What had the website said? Redefine your future in three days, something like that. Discover new possibility. Well, OK, good. It would be a pleasure.

But she didn't relish the thought of the nametags. Or the tearful disclosure of personal stories. She didn't know if such storytelling would occur, Marnie had never told her how it worked, but that was the way she pictured it.

Marnie didn't even know about Lynn. Had never met him or even heard of him. Marnie would never know what she'd lost.

She was going in her front door when her cell rang: the vampire was calling. She was so tired. She almost didn't pick up.

"So did they make an offer? The Chinese?"

"Not yet," said Nina, dropping her bag on a chair and moving through the living room to the kitchen. She'd have to open a new bottle for her evening glass; she grabbed one from the fridge door, phone couched awkwardly between her ear and shoulder. "They're considering it as an investment, but there's no offer yet. I would have called if there had been, of course."

"Yeah. I guess you would."

"I can tell you right now, if they do make an offer they won't be meeting your asking."

"I know. We counter, then we compromise. I know the drill."

Pause. Nina had learned not to speak into the silence of clients.

"So, my freezer. I left it unlocked."

"I noticed that," said Nina.

"I was so, so late," said the vampire. "The alarm like didn't go off at all."

"Well, I locked it," said Nina. She put down the bottle because her neck was hurting.

"Did you look?"

Now was the time to lie; anyone would. But honestly, she could stand to lose the listing. Let someone else sell the taxidermy bats. A shame, right when she had the first serious interest. But still. It wouldn't be the only time she put in legwork and got zero payout.

"I did," she said. "Rats. Squirrels. A tabby cat. Is that legal?"

"You weren't supposed to look."

"The buyers were late and I was doing cleanup in the kitchen. I do apologize."

There was a long pause. In the background, Nina heard music.

"Look, I used to be a purist," said the vampire. "Human blood only, right? That's the mainstream. But I branched out recently."

"OK," said Nina.

"It's thinking outside the box. That's all."

"I'm not judging," said Nina.

"All right. So let me know if they make an offer."

She hung up without answering the question about dead cats.

Half relief, half disappointment. Maybe the vampire planned to drink her blood later.

She uncorked the wine, poured a glass and went into her bedroom, stood before the altar. Looked at his picture and felt that she'd never deserved him. She'd said to the therapist, full of pathetic self-pity, "The world knew that. So it took him from me."

"Right," said the therapist. "Because the world revolves around you." She'd been properly shamed.

She knew it, when she thought logically. No one had singled her out.

But when she lay alone in her bed, she saw the cold symmetry. She saw the balancing of the scales.

Tonight's line came from a dog-eared anthology of war poets, its ruff of yellow page edges softened by his hands. Some evenings she tucked it under her pillow. When she wanted to go to sleep but couldn't, she lay thinking of his face. How it could never be repeated. There might be similar faces, the curve of a lip that was the same, a rough approximation of features. Never the whole.

And the face was fading. She looked at his picture to remind herself, but still it was fading.

What had been behind the face, though. That didn't fade so easily. The invisible part she wouldn't forget.

"Whatever hope is yours, is my life also," she quoted, and drank. For all the wine he'd never drink.

Her phone rang again. She heard it in the kitchen and hurried out of her room to check it: the woman with the midgets. Felt a bit unsteady as she hit accept. She should drink less. Eat more. Lost fifteen pounds since the accident.

"I went to the house!" said Delia. "I got this feeling, like I had to say goodbye to it. Like face my fear. So I drove up. And there was a light on. In the attic! Because they were there!"

"OK," said Nina warily.

"I swear! No one believes me. They were there! You have to go over. You have to see them! They're squatters!"

"But even if I did," said Nina, "what would that do?"

"Please," said the woman. "Please. I even took a picture! I took a picture of them!"

"You should call the police," said Nina. "If there are really illegal squatters in the house, then you should call."

She couldn't drive right now. Unfit. Certainly not at the whim of a disturbed client.

"Could you call, then? At least call the police for me?"

That she could do. If it would soothe the woman.

"I'll report it for you. Yes."

They hung up, Delia still agitated. Was it worth a 911? No. Call the local precinct.

She looked up the number, called it in. The dispatch said they'd send a squad car over.

It wasn't till later, when she was getting ready for bed, that she got a text ping. Delia again. She swiped and looked at the photo. Enlarged it. Just the dim outline of a roof, and in the center a small square of yellow light.

STOCKHOLM

They had some Swedish chick lined up to be the au pair, all qualified and shit. A grad student in child development. But she bailed at the last minute. Back in Sweden her mother got leukemia. Was that the country where they all wore clogs? Lexie pictured the mother, bald and clog-dancing sadly in some tulips. Wearing a chemo turban. But Google said tulips and clogs were Dutch—a country with dams they called dikes, which a boy once put his finger in. No joke. They had a legend about it. People rode bicycles. And drove clown cars.

Holland looked lame on Google, like a creepy fairy tale with all the tulips and windmills, but Sweden seemed normal. And friendly. Probably had to be, so people would keep living there when it was shit-cold all the time.

Jem told her the au pair thing would be a sweet deal. The house was killer, the food was free, and how much work could a new baby be? She'd babysat a couple of babies. They didn't do much for the first four months, basically lay there. Sometimes crying. When you picked them up, you had to support their heads. Their necks were rubbery. If you didn't hold up the heads they could roll back. And then what? Would the babies strangulate? She looked it up. Enh. Didn't happen that much. Their deal was sleep, cry, drink milk, shit. The baby shit barely even smelled bad, people said. Looked like mustard.

After that she figured she'd cut out anyway, get her own place. Six months max. When babies turned six months old they started to do stuff. She didn't want to be around for that.

He said to tell them, when she called to set up the interview, that she had trouble at home. Which was true: a perv stepfather counted as trouble. Jem's dad's new wife would give her points for that. Like, she'd count as help for the baby, but also count as charity. Fine. The wife was a ditz but pretty nice, said Jem, and also might have come from a sketchy background, since his dad had picked her up in a strip club. He said to act innocent and mega-sincere, but tell them she'd helped to raise her brothers.

And she had, if stepbrothers counted. Who were older than you and ran a pretty decent-sized meth business. A few times she'd had to slap them down. That counted as helping to raise, didn't it? She'd taught them a lesson or two.

She wanted to be an actress, so act, said Jem. You dream of being a theater major. Maybe UCLA. It's hypothetical, said Jem. He used big words.

His grandma was a risk factor. He said she used to be a professor, was perceptive and could smell bullshit. Also, don't fuck with her, he said. He was fond of the old lady. I want her taken care of, he said. With her, don't be fake Christian, she's Jewish, well, kind of, but she was raised by some kind of missionaries so she'll see through it. Tell her about your trashy family. I mean, don't mention the Internet sex biz, that being how we met and shit, but other than that, just try to be a straight shooter. She won't mind the white-trash part, as long as you're smart and not rude. She likes an edge but she really doesn't like rudeness. Treat her with respect, she's had a hard life. Her whole family died in the Holocaust when she was six.

Plus her husband, Jem's grandpa and also a Holocaust survivor, had offed himself in aught-6. One of those car-in-the-garage situations. Jem's parents had told him it was a stroke at the time, he was only seven then, but later he found out the deal.

So she hitched a ride down from Carpinteria with some friends going to a concert, not to cut into her savings. For the interview she wore a preppie, baby-blue button-down shirt with flat-zero sex appeal. And a necklace with a small cross on it, to show she was wholesome. She put her fingers on the cross when she was asked a personal question, kind of suggesting it meant security, plus that she loved the baby Jesus. She also learned a bunch of quotes from the Bible. Well, three. She tried to find ones about being nice to kids, but the Bible wasn't into that.

"Children are a gift from the Lord," was the best quote, which she trotted out in the interview. She got it from an embroidered cushion in a thrift store, but Googled it and it was in the Bible all right. In the Psalms part. She mentioned that to Jem and it was a good thing she did, because he told her you didn't pronounce the *P*.

Rookie mistake, he said.

His dad and Lora weren't religious, Jem said, but they'd feel

safe with a Christian girl around the house. Christian was short
for boring. "*Ergo*, safe," said Jem. Lora was pretty distracted by
the baby coming out soon. Obsessively rubbing cream on her
stomach to fight off stretch marks. But she seemed to like Lexie
OK. All Lexie had to do was take a course in infant CPR. They'd
pay. And the references were no problem, she gave them friends'
phone numbers and one number of an actual woman she used to
babysit for, before she found faster ways to make money.

With Lora and Paul the act was Nice Girl, which she'd done
plenty of times on camera, minus the full-frontal and grinding.

The grandma was for sure a harder nut to crack. With her she
also did Nice Girl, and tried to speak correctly. Nice Girl but kind
of damaged. Which she was, technically, due to the acts of Stepdad Pete. She wouldn't pass the virgin test. No blood on the white
sheets. The grandma didn't drive much anymore, but still owned
a car, which she let her use for errands. On her days off too, the
lady said, she could use it, and also said to call her Aleska.

She checked with Jem: it wasn't the one his grandpa had sui-
cided in. Though she would've driven the shit out of it anyway.

Jem said she'd be his mole. She'd feed him information on his
dad. Not clear what. Point was, he couldn't stand the guy. Mumbled about wanting to force him to give more money to his mom.
She'd had to downsize big-time after the divorce. Even though
she got alimony and all that, they still had to leave their swank
pad in the Hills for a regular house. It was from the eighties and
uber-ugly, but had a decent view of the Silver Lake Reservoir, he
said. But he wanted his mother to get more. Plus his dad should
be punished. With extreme prejudice, he said.

The room was private, with its own bath and entrance and even
a lock on the other door, the one that opened to the rest of the

house. So she could keep her business going. Plus the Wi-Fi was faster than her setup back home, where she'd had to make out with the Comcast guy for an upgrade because Perv Pete was such a cheapskate. She kept that sideline to the nights though, times when she was sure she wouldn't be interrupted. You'd lose repeat customers if you stopped what you were doing, in those scenarios.

She and Lora were putting finishing touches on the nursery, four days into her stay—Lora was rearranging a shelf of stuffed animals and Lexie was basically just watching and sometimes going, "Oh that's so cute! The koala bear's my favorite!"—when she looked down and saw her foot, her own foot with nothing covering it but a pink flip-flop, and the flip-flop was standing in a puddle. She thought Lora had peed herself, the baby pressing on her bladder, which Lora complained about six times a day, but only for a second.

"OMG! I'm so sorry," said Lora. "Call Paul! Would you?"

When he pulled up in his car to get her, Lexie handed him the hospital bag, prepared weeks before, and said cheerily, "I hope it all goes great! I'll pray on it!"

After they drove off she was home-free, just had to check in on Aleska. She fixed her a sandwich, pastrami and Swiss on toasted marble rye the way she liked it, then grabbed a diet soda from the fridge and went back to her room, where she chalked up two sessions back to back. The first was with an old geezer in Sherman Oaks who paid for a Coy Cheerleader but ended up crying over his dead wife, and the second was with a closeted lesbian in Texas. The closeted part was obvious because she was using her husband's credit card—had barely heard of Paypal. How did these people stay so clueless?

It wouldn't be a problem, Lexie reassured her: the name of the business was Organic Natural Cosmetics, and that was the line item that would appear on the statement. She was a professional small-business owner, she took care of business. The closeted lesbian asked for Slutty Schoolgirl, gay version, which Lexie did exactly like she did the straight version, except with a different script and extra props.

Then she messaged Jem and told him his baby half-sister was coming. *Felicitations*, she wrote, since he liked long words.

Break out the monster spliffs, he texted back.

She wouldn't do him IRL any more than she would the geezer with the dead wife, mostly the zits would be the problem, plus he was hella gangly—a human spider with acne. But he was a friend, more or less. Only a friend would set you up in a gig like this. A rich kid, yeah, but he somewhat knew how shit went down. She'd promised him freebies online, but it was pretty much a joke, they'd stopped that after they met face to face. Plus she was living with his family now, or part of it. Anyway free online sex was an expanding universe. Went on and on forever. Only rubes paid for it, or people who didn't care about money. And that wasn't Jem anymore: he'd stopped abusing his mother's plastic. Something about dignity, although he said it in ancient Greek. *Dignitas* something something. Certified nerd.

Aleska buzzed on the intercom and said there was a guest coming over. Would Lexie "be so kind as to" listen for the door and bring her on back? So she couldn't book more sessions. Then Paul texted that Lora was "still only two centimeters dilated." TMI. Plus why centimeters? Why was it the metric system all of a sudden, as soon as you talked about somebody's hooha opening up to squeeze out a baby? The only time she ever heard it. You wouldn't use it in porn, that was for sure. "Come on, baby.

Shove those fourteen centimeters inside me." Wouldn't get far with that.

Guys liked to hear inches. Some liked a two-way feed, so she had something to go on. But it didn't make a difference, really. You had to say eight inches minimum, even sight unseen. The dumber they were, the more inches they wanted to hear. That was a rule of thumb.

Doorbell. She put on her Nice Girl face and went to answer it.

A woman stood there, pretty and put-together but mega-sad. The sadness was all over her like sand was on the beach.

"You're here for Aleska, right? My name's Lexie. I'm the au pair."

"Nina," said the woman, and reached out to shake her hand.

For a second Lexie wanted to hold it. Weird. She never held her mother's hand. Couldn't remember ever holding it. Her mother's nails were too long: she was proud of them. She got manicures every week. It was all about the nails.

"Cool. Come on back."

"Nina? Welcome. She's going to sell my house for me," said Aleska, when they went into the cottage. You had to knock and go in; if she was sitting at her desk, which she usually was, Aleska didn't get up.

"Oh, right," said Lexie. "You love that house."

Shit, she'd said the wrong thing. Aleska's face looked fallen in. But she mustered a smile.

"I do," she said softly. "That house is my baby."

No wonder, because Paul wasn't much to brag about. Aleska, all elegant and refined, had to be bummed about having a son who was your basic Beamer-driving asshole. He texted and played phone games at the dinner table, which OK, maybe was normal some places, such as at her mom's, but she saw a look of horror on Aleska's face. Plus he made Lora wash her coochie right in front of him, with antibacterial soap, before he'd go down on her. He had to see firsthand that it was sparkling clean. That was a bonus about Lora: she talked about everything. No boundaries. Or self-respect. By Day Two she'd already told Lexie half the secrets of her sex life. Apparently not knowing they were kind of pathetic.

But she was nice. That counted for a lot.

At least, unlike Pete the Perv, Paul didn't seem to have a weakness for teens. He'd never looked at her sideways. Although she hadn't stress-tested him, hadn't wandered out of her bedroom in her gauzy thong so he could get a gander at her well-kept Brazilian-plus-landing strip. She didn't dare risk it, though she was curious if he would pass or fail. But curiosity killed the cat. Anyway she sensed his natural cutoff was somewhere around drinking age. It showed in how he didn't ogle her. He was a lech, given Lora had half his years and probably half his IQ, but not a perv. So you could say two good things about Paul: he was rich and not a pedophile. Both were advantages he had over Pete. Go Paul!

"I think I may understand," said Nina. "I recently had to sell a house that belonged to someone I was close to. Who died suddenly. There was a lot of emotion."

There it was: the sadness.

Aleska gazed at her thoughtfully, nodding.

"I'll leave you guys in peace," said Lexie. "Oh. And Paul texted me. He said, um, she's only two centimeters dilated?"

"Good gracious," said Aleska crabbily. "Why people think we need to know these details. It really is beyond me. You can spare me the 3-4-5 updates, dear. I only wish my son would spare you."

Lexie fixed a club soda with lime for Nina and left the cottage just as Jem texted he was out front. His new tactic with the dad was Nice Guy, which Paul was too thick to see for the act it was. So for the birth of his half-sister he was bringing over a gift. He'd leave it. Wouldn't hang around. It was a giant purple teddy bear with crazy eyes. He'd won it, he said, in a shooting game at the Santa Monica Pier. High as a kite.

"I even bought a card," he said, and showed her the envelope, which had *For My Baby Sister* written on it in a flowing script. He'd drawn hearts and flowers around the words. They were obviously ironic, but Paul wouldn't look and Lora wouldn't suspect.

His mom, he'd said, was wrecked by the whole baby thing. She'd wanted another kid after Jem, kind of wanted to have a boy and a girl, but Paul had said no. One was more than enough, he said. Then he went and knocked up Lora on the side, and meanwhile Jem's mom was too old now, her eggs all dried up like they got.

She showed him her room, which he hadn't seen before. "Not bad," he said curtly. "Beats mine hands-down. Thing's the size of a closet. And not a walk-in, either. You're high on the hog here, Lexie."

"Only because of you," she said.

Home was a pit. The apartment always smells like stepdad B.O. and old beer. One thousand spilled PBRs must have soaked into the shag. and her mother went crazy with the Febreze. That was the third smell: B.O., stale beer and Febreze.

"Yeah, no worries."

"You and Aleska getting along?"

He picked up a vase from a shelf. Not hers, of course. Square, glass and modern-looking. It came with the room. Some twigs were sitting in it. On purpose. Around the house there were a bunch of vases with nothing in them but bare sticks.

"I think so. I can't tell if she likes me, but she's cool. I make her favorite sandwiches for lunch, with pickles on the side. And I pour her drinks stiff."

Jem nodded jerkily. Awkward fucking guy. He put the vase back carefully. For a second she'd thought he might drop it. What stepbro Ely would've done—he lived to smash up shit. Whenever something looked breakable, Ely wanted to break it.

"The way she likes 'em," he said.

"Two measures," said Lexie.

Jem had his hands shoved down in his pants pockets and was avoiding her eyes. Embarrassing, them standing like this. Next to her bed.

"You want to go back and say hi?" she asked. "There's a real-estate agent here. To talk about selling her house."

He shrugged.

"In a while."

"OK."

Was she supposed to offer him sex? Was there a bill coming due? Maybe she'd assumed wrong. She'd never had actual sex in trade for favors. The Comcast guy, that was just face. And tits. Pete didn't count.

But nothing was free. And every guy wanted it.

Small panic. She'd do it. If it meant staying here.

"Hey. Jem. Is there . . . do you need anything? From me?"

Smooth, Lexie. Smooth.

He turned to the window, looked out at the neighbor's hedge. There was a hummingbird feeder in a gap and as they watched a bird hovered, dipped its tiny beak. Flew away.

"Nah, I'm good. Let's take the home tour," he said.

Relief.

She never went into the master except at Lora's invitation, but Jem led the way. The bed was made—a big gold thing, four-poster and angular—and the room was neat. The housekeeper's work, since Lora tended to drop her clothes wherever she changed and leave them lying there. Dolores went around picking up after her. One wall was sliding doors to a private patio, and opposite the bed their massive TV was sunk into the wall.

"Dad's stuff," said Jem, and opened some drawers in a nightstand. "He always takes this side. Score! The blue pills."

He raised a Viagra box.

"But every guy his age pops these," said Jem. "Not blackmail material." He tossed the package back in and kept rummaging. Pulled out a set of handcuffs.

"Better," said Lexie. "Right?"

She felt kind of nervous, but then: only two centimeters.

Still, she sneaked a glance over her shoulder.

"Who wears them, him or her?"

"Him, for sure," she said. "It's his idea and he wears them. If it was her—too obvious."

"True dat, the girl's already cuffed and stuffed," said Jem. "In jail for life, baby mama."

"What's this?" he asked, holding up a small chain.

"Nipple clamps," said Lexie.

"You're an old hand." He put them back and picked up a leather billfold now, thin and worn. Flipped it open.

"No cash," he said. Then pulled something out of one of the folds: a photo. She leaned in to see. A toddler boy holding a red alphabet block with the letter *J.*

"It's you," she said.

Jem stared at it.

"He keeps a picture of me with the sex props," he said. "That's twisted."

"Or maybe he just looks at it sometimes."

"No way. This photo hasn't seen the light of day for years. He forgot it's in here. Guaranteed."

He shoved the picture in his pants pocket and tossed the wallet back in the drawer.

"Should you—"

"He'll never know it's gone. Let's book."

Text from Aleska. Could Lexie bring back white wine from the wine refrigerator? *Choose an expensive bottle*, she wrote.

"Gotta get some wine for your grandmother."

"She doesn't drink wine. Hard liquor only," said Jem.

"It's probably for the real estate lady? Right?"

"Same one that sold our house, I bet," said Jem. "Heard my moms on the phone. Recommending."

One bottle still had a price tag on it, eighty bucks. She figured that should qualify and headed for the back-door sliders. Jem lingered behind.

"You don't want to come back?"

"Later," he mumbled, and threw himself down on the couch. Closed his eyes.

In the cottage Nina was settled in an armchair. Aleska had moved into another one—rare that she left her desk.

"Could you pour a glass for Nina, dear?" she asked.

She couldn't pretend she didn't know her way around a corkscrew. Pete was a beer-and-whiskey man, but her mother drank two-buck Chuck. She weighed maybe a hundred pounds and lived off Dr Pepper and curly fries. Usually too wasted by the first bottle to open the second. Lexie'd been uncorking them at the ripe old age of twelve. A preteen sommelier. Pervy Pete called her that. But now her mom drank screw-top or box. She and Pete would fall asleep on the ancient recliner, Mom on Peter's lap, half their clothes off. Mom, stretch marks. Pete, hairy ass and thighs. Snoring.

Q: Did the widdle girl miss her mommy?

A: Not really.

Blackmail material, Jem'd said. Did he mean it? Probably running his mouth. He was pissed, but come on. He might be smart and have half a clue, but like all rich kids, when push came to shove he didn't know how good he had it.

It was like: Don't rock the boat, man. Don't screw me over.

C-section, texted Paul.

"C-section," read Lexie, and handed Nina her wine.

"Of course," said Aleska. "They're always in a rush. Just cut her open. Like Caligula. Fix me a drink too, will you, Lexie? The hour is upon us, thank God."

"Sure," said Lexie, and reached for the Hendrick's.

"Do you mind if I ask you a personal question?"

"Um, no," she said, surprised, pouring.

"You dropped out of high school, is that correct?"

"Yeah," said Lexie. "I didn't like going there. I did a GED instead."

"I'm taking an informal poll. You see that poster there? Above my desk?"

You couldn't miss it. Thing had a big-ass swastika. German words about triumph. Lexie nodded.

"What did that illustrate, do you think?"

"Like . . . a Nazi rally?"

"And that one. Who's in that picture over there?" Aleska pointed. Her hand shook as she lowered it again, the fingers slender and bony. One graceful silver ring. Or maybe platinum. Sparkling with small jewels.

"Papa Joe Stalin," said Lexie promptly.

Perv Pete fancied himself a WWII buff. He liked to talk about the firebombing of Dresden over pepperoni pizza. He said, "Twenty-five thousand burned alive in one night. Women and children. Thanks to Uncle Sam." He said, "Yeah, that's right. 9/11 wasn't *shit*."

"Thank you, my dear. I knew I could count on you. Will you take a drink yourself?"

"I'm only seventeen," said Lexie.

"We used to drink watered wine at dinner," mused Aleska. "As children. I don't think it stunted our growth. Hard to tell, though. We were all undersized."

"My parents are lushes. My mom and stepdad. So I never got into it."

"Have a splash of the white. If you don't like it, you can just dump the rest. Sit down with us a while. Won't you?"

"OK. Yes. Thank you."

She poured a little wine, took a cautious sip. It tasted sour. Not good, but not that bad.

"Your father isn't in the picture, I gather?" said Aleska. She had a way of asking prying questions that sounded totally polite. The way she said it, it almost sounded like: hey. It'd be rude of her *not* to ask.

"He took off when I was in kindergarten. Then, like, later—I think I was in maybe sixth grade?—he ended up in prison. For lame stuff, Spam scams or phishing. Fraud I guess. He was at Lompoc? Near the big fields of flowers?"

"I'm not familiar with that particular prison," said Aleska.

"You can see the flowers right from the road. Anyway it's low-security but someone beat him up in there. Some white-power dude. Head injuries. He got kinda brain-damaged after that."

"I'm sorry," said Aleska.

"No sweat," said Lexie. She sipped the wine. "Like you said, right? He's out of the picture. I barely remember what he looks like anymore."

They were quiet for a minute. Had Jem fallen asleep, back in there on the couch? Jem liked to sleep.

"Sounds like you had it rough," said Nina.

"Not like Aleska did," said Lexie. Was that allowed? Was she supposed to say it? The wine was already making her say stuff. Jem liked to say *in vino veritas*. His whole dead-language deal.

"Ancient history, dear. As it happens, none of us in this room really grew up with fathers," said Aleska. "Although—your step-dad? Was he any help?"

"I wouldn't say that," said Lexie. Pete standing, boozy and swaying, at the door to her room. One time, the side of his head crushing her face, she tasted greasy hair and earwax.

"To the fatherless children," said Nina quietly, and lifted her wineglass. Lexie must have been staring at the floor, because when she looked at Nina with the glass raised she was still thinking of it. Like the spot seared into your eyeball if you looked at the sun, except it wasn't bright. It was dim. A gray rug with a pattern of blue flowers.

Pete's exit line: Don't hurt your mother, now. Don't ever hurt your mother, kid.

He took the low road, Pete.

"The lost children," said Aleska, and drank.

Did they mean her?

Jun, her only real friend at school, had been adopted from China when she was a baby. It wasn't fair, Lexie had thought when she listened to Jun's parents tell her adoption story at their dinner table once, how those adopting parents had to pass a gazillion tests to get a kid to take care of, but people pumping out their own babies didn't have to pass jack shit. You had to take a bunch of tests to help a kid that needed you, but not to make a brand-new kid you'd warp for twenty years. Or more.

Jem was rapping at the door.

He must have got bored.

"Come in, dear," said Aleska. "Have a drink."

"We're drinking," said Lexie. Like an idiot.

"A celebration," said Aleska. "Of the new baby."

Jem stepped in, nodded briefly at Nina, walked over and bent to kiss his grandma on the cheek.

"You got any Glenlivet?" he asked.

"Something like it," said Aleska, and waved her hand at the bar. Jem started opening cabinets.

"So," said Aleska. "Jem. Lexie. How did the two of you meet?"

"Oh. Just online," said Lexie. *Shit.*

"You mean, one of those online dating services?" asked Aleska. "They're popular, I hear."

"Gram. We're not *dating*. Jesus," said Jem.

"We're just friends," said Lexie. "It was more of a chatroom deal." Not completely a lie. They *had* chatted. And been in rooms.

"A chatroom. Like, for troubled teens," said Jem. He held the whiskey bottle but didn't pour. Kind of frozen.

"For *troubled teens*?" repeated Aleska. Skeptical. No wonder. Jem had never said "troubled teens" in his whole life.

"Everyone seems to meet on social networking sites these

days," said Nina to Aleska. "When I was coming up, there was no way to meet new people. I mean. Except school or the neighborhood. You had to take what was there. Or leave it. Now—there are downsides, but at least it expands their social possibilities."

Nina to the rescue! Whoa. Thanks, Nina.

Jem shot the woman a startled look, but she didn't meet his eyes, just took a dainty sip of her drink.

"So what are they naming the baby girl?" she asked.

"Aubree?" said Jem, turning back to the bar, and poured himself way too much whiskey. An inch from the rim, like it was orange juice. Had he even drunk his very own glass of whiskey before? Didn't appear that way. She wanted to say, Jem, two fingers, man. Be cool. "Madison? Kinsley?"

"Oh dear. I do hope not," said Aleska.

"Too nineties," said Lexie.

"Or eighties," said Nina.

"We had a lot of Tammis," said Lexie. "In my class once there were three Tammis. And a Pammi."

They were shooting the shit after that. The wine started to taste OK. She let Jem get her a second glass. Nudged by Aleska, of course. He wouldn't have thought of it.

The buzz was lighter than pot, not as sleepy. But less fun than coke. She'd never tried Ely's meth. One look at the skanks that did it was enough. Plus Toff, for some reason, didn't want her to. It wasn't a clean high, he said. That was the nicest he'd ever been, not wanting his stepsister to do his meth.

"I should get used to the Madisons. Mom wants me to go to some private school for senior year," said Jem. Unexpected.

"What do *you* want?" asked Aleska.

Jem shrugged.

"Don't care," he said. "She's really into it. I warned her I couldn't get in anyway. My grades are kinda crap. Some, anyway. Plus I cut all the time. But she said her friend's on some committee and owes her a major favor. They went to high school together back East. She showed me old pictures. It's like, this New York all-girls school? That's been there like, forever? Get this: their mascot is a beaver."

Lexie laughed.

"Slang," said Jem to Aleska. "Don't worry about it."

He seemed relaxed. Probably the booze, but as she looked at him she thought: what he needed was company. If she was his friend, like if they hung out and did shit together, there was a chance he wouldn't bother messing with his dad. Wouldn't want to. He might let it go, even. There might be calm seas.

She could stay on here. Maybe a whole year. Maybe two.

Sex was too obvious. Plus it could backfire. She'd been thinking too small. Selfish. Like, wanting control. It wasn't cool.

"You should go," she said. "Mix it up. It's not like you *like* being where you are."

"Yeah," said Jem, and swirled the whiskey around in his glass. "Whatever. You know. Whatever makes her happy."

He loved his mom. She should love hers. Shouldn't she?

But Pete had blocked out her mother. And her mother had no clue. She knew Lexie wasn't there, but she didn't know why.

Pete rubbed off all over everything. She used to tell her mother stuff. But since he started up, she never did. Couldn't. Too much in the way. Because Pete was the truth and she couldn't tell it. And she used to be all her mother had. "You're the only good thing I ever did," she always said. Not fair. It wasn't fair to her mother. Her mother didn't understand. Couldn't.

The night before she left her mother'd wanted to talk but *she* hadn't wanted to. Because she never did anymore. So they just sat there on the sofa, her channel-surfing and her mother clicking through kitten and puppy pictures on her phone. Her favorite pet celebrity: Grumpy Cat. Clicking, clicking. "Look. Isn't he so funny?" But Lexie'd just rolled her eyes, changed the channel again, not even looked. She hadn't even *looked* at Grumpy Cat.

All she felt for her mother was pity. Feeling it was terrible. She didn't want to. She didn't want to feel it.

She could try harder, now that she wasn't living at home. Now that he wasn't on her. She could be nicer from far away.

But could you just decide? To make love come back?

I CAN'T GO ON

She didn't tell her mother where she was. She said she was fine, she said she was "awesome." But not where.

Rita had been upset at first, sure, she got sad. She was sad for a couple weeks. Maybe a few. But she texted Lexie a lot and Lexie sent back perky little texts like *Everythings cool, XoJ*. Or *Im serious, Im doing great*. So Rita was OK. She had a teary moment or two, times when she said, My baby girl! Out there alone!

But basically, she was OK.

He wasn't. Not at all. He missed her like a knife in the gut. It didn't go away.

Most nights he burrowed into Rita. Dutiful husband. Worked best in the beat-up Naugahyde recliner, where he could look at

the row of school pictures over Rita's shoulder while she strad-
dled him. Portraits, one from each year. They were in frames with
hearts and roses on them. All pictures of the girl. His own boys
never used to show up for crap like that—school picture day, all
that bullshit. So there were no pictures of Ely and Toff's surly
faces to wilt his dick.

He'd look straight at the pictures when Rita was on him.
Things were right with the universe, at those moments. Well no.
OK. The universe was a 24/7 shitshow. But at least there was order
in the sex. Chair, photos in a row. The angles worked.

Rita was solid. She held up her end and she liked to get laid.
Couldn't say that for all women. He'd met her in a fucking *mall*,
been at Sears looking at appliances, and she was walking along
holding Lexie's little hand. Rita dropped some bags, spilled little-
girl clothes out, and he was right there so he helped her pick them
up. They went to the food court, where Lexie had a milkshake
and Rita said he looked like an actor. Some guy who played a
Mormon on TV. Lexie was eight then. He'd just thought she was
cute. *Cute kid*, he said to Rita.

Rita meant well. But he always thought of Lexiegirl when it
was time to come. Not Lexie: Lexie was her civilian name. Lexiegirl. What he used to call her out loud, a long, long time ago.
Before he even slipped a finger in.

He didn't think of her right off the bat when he and Rita did
it. Out of respect. He waited till Rita was done. Or maybe till she
dozed off. Happened sometimes. They liked to drink and they
weren't young. He had the timing down pat. Stroke, stroke, sweet
fuzzy snatch. Stroke, stroke, little round tits. Then it was fast.
Hard. It made him roar, sometimes. Ragged throat noise.

Rita took it as a compliment.

There was guilt, sure, a small tug when he remembered times Lexiegirl had tried to put him off. It lay there till he drank and shut down the memory flashes. Why he'd waited for her to turn sixteen. He kept a silent promise. Sixteen: whatever the law said, come on, it was just a fact, girls turned to women then. In Mexico, the girls turned fifteen and they called it good. The Mexicans were smart. Hard workers and smart about women. Those waiting years, they'd been shit tough. But he was strong. He held fast, he waited. Every birthday after twelve—she got her period that year—there he was, counting down the clock. In some countries, girls got married off at twelve. Shit, ten.

This was a fucked-up place, land of the Puritans. Land of repressed bullshit. One rule for the masters, another for the slaves. Three hundred million hypocrites. Bomb kids in brown countries. Tens of thousands. Drones manned by pimply button-pushers at Langley or Creech blew up shit-tons of Arab babies. Just blew those babies to fucking smithereens. Have these ones, heaven! Muslim babies, stone-dead! You like 'em, God? We chose 'em just for you!

Nice work, soldier. Hey, job well done. Back pat. Or shoulder, maybe. Pat-pat. Bond-bond. Brothers in arms.

Then preach about age of consent. Do as I say, not as I do. Respect life! Holier-than-thou motherfuckers. So fucking holy.

He had photos, but none naked. His best was her in a yellow bikini. Three summers back. She was fourteen. He'd jumped through hoops to get it printed out. Rita kept all her snaps of Lexie on her phone. Be weird to ask her to forward them with no reason. He had to make up a family album project. That Christmas. Said he'd order a photo calendar. And he did. Website. Easy. Then printed out a dozen just of Lexiegirl in her bikini. She was standing with friends, one fat, the other Chinese. Cropped the shit out of them. Gone, girls, he said as he did it. Fuck off, Fatty and Chink. Felt a bit bad thinking that, those girls were OK kids, he drove them to the pool himself that time, all giggling in the back about some picture of an obscene cupcake on Instagram, but shit, your head went where it went.

Kept the dozen printouts in his office safe. Did all his personal business in that office. After hours. Pulled down the blinds. Locked the door. And went for it. Just went for it.

Highlight of every day. Saved it up till it was like a sunburst. Plasma exploding. At the last moment he squeezed his eyes shut. His eyes behind the eyelids felt black-hot.

When one copy got worn out, he burned it in an ashtray and broke out the next.

Variety, though. You needed it. One other photo that he liked, she had clothes on but was leaning forward and you saw cleavage. Made six copies of that. It got him off but it was frustrating. Where were the peachy thighs? Where was the belly button? The Zero G ripe ass? No dimples. No sag. Mostly, where was the luscious cunt? Nothing as good as that. In the bikini picture, you could see everything frontal but the triangle. Even the nipples were there, wet pale fabric of the bra cups showing their shadows.

He missed her smell. Her smell was what he missed and had no way of getting near. He had some dirty panties but the scent faded to nothing over time. Used to bury his face in her. Best time was one weekend when Rita went off to a workshop overnight. Simi Valley. Like, self-help. Self-improvement. He thought, improve *my*self. That time he was in with her for hours. Not minutes. Still remembered the date. Weather, even. Dinner. Microwave chicken burrito with cheese. Brushed his teeth, Listerine Original, showered. The T-shirt she was wearing. It said pink. Shit yeah. He went down on her like there was nowhere else. And there wasn't. Core of the world.

She came that time. He could swear it. She didn't want to but she did. She came on his mouth and he wished never to wash it. Could go around with that all day.

He tried to find the smell in Rita. They had the same genes, didn't they? A lot of the same, anyway. Half. The faintest reminder. Not similar at all.

He needed to decouple. Lexiegirl from Rita. Slot in the new one where she used to fit.

But he couldn't stand to. He tried. He saw some on the streets. Some tweenie shows on cable. One actress on one stupid show he thought had decent potential. They trotted them out in barely any clothes. She had those pouty lips. Reminded him. He tried. But in the end, nope, no cigar. Computer no use, obviously. FBI. NSA. Anyway. Fruitless. For now. Brain was locked. Circuits wired. He wouldn't give up hope. The world would beat her down. She'd come back. She was seventeen. Well, almost eighteen. Almost legal. And shit-poor.

That was good, picturing her return. Come back begging. You'll beg for it, he told the picture, sitting at his office desk. Beating off. Take me back, Daddy Pete.

Two months in, Rita, messing with her phone one night over pizza, suddenly squealed and said: "Oh look! Wow! I didn't know I still had this. Look! I'm still paying her phone bills. She's on my account, and that app you put on both our phones that time? She still has it. The GPS shows her. It shows right where she is! Look, Lexie's in L.A.!"

Almost lost it. Pulse racing. Numb face. Had the weird sensation his lips were a slab of meat. Meat with meat inside. Well shit, yeah. They were. Hands shook. Sat there steady, kept his shaking hands beneath the table edge. Then: "Hey, I could have told you that—I didn't know we were still paying. It's cool, though. Yeah, that's fine. Nice part of town? Let's see. Oh yeah, Brentwood. Real safe neighborhood."

A dot. The actual street address. Blazed on his memory.

So then, four days later—had to wait so it didn't seem related— he had a business trip, he told Rita. Pick up some wholesale from a warehouse. Riverside, he mentioned. Snagged a baggie of coke from Ely's private stash. Ely sold meth but never touched the stuff: for personal use, cocaine and oxy were the choice poisons. He'd switched out his regular work truck with the one Rubio liked to use, left the keys on the hook with a note saying he needed the extra space. Didn't want Lexie to see him coming. Cranked up his music in the cab. Old stuff he liked from way back when. As a young buck. Swinging testes. AC/DC, Motörhead. "The chase is better than the catch." Barreling down the 5.

When he switched to the radio, some newer crap came on. "I can't go on, I go on." Lame ska punk or something. Switched back to the USB.

Driving into the city was an adrenaline rush. Off the free-way, coming into the neighborhood, he rolled slow on the dark, curving streets. Even so, had to pull over twice. First let himself calm down, then did a little blow. First thing was to observe. It was 1 a.m. He found the house, drove past and circled back. Not much street parking. Signs posted. Meant not much cover, no other vehicles at the curb. That bit. She didn't know the truck, but it was out of place. Plus, high-class neighborhood. Garages. Big houses. Hers was behind a gate *and* a hedge. Not one but

both. How'd she gotten *this* fucking gig? Young people didn't live
in houses like this. Sure as shit wasn't a rental. Was she living off
some other horny middle-aged fuck?

He had questions. Man did he have questions. Maybe sleep
a bit, though. Coke wearing off. He was tired. Could he sleep
here? Would there be a rat-a-tat-tat on the driver's side window?
Private-security patrolling? Far from impossible. Likely. OK.
New plan: sleep in the truck on San Vicente. Set the phone
alarm. No one would be up before six. Except maybe some ille-
gals doing yard work. Come back, park under that big tree.
Watch, wait, see what he'd see.

Alarm was the sound of a cricket. Barely made noise. He fumbled for the phone. OK. Up. Did a line. Water on face from a
bottle rolling around on the floor. Fuzzy mouth. Was there gum?
Rubio was always chewing a wad. He popped the glove. Nicotine
gum, that was it. Fine. Still minty, right? He tore a piece from the
foil. Hard. Hands trembling.

He pulled up the GPS and headed out, was on her street and
rolling past, didn't have a new plan formed, just rolling past the
house to scope it out by day. And shit, the luck of the fucking
Irish. Damn if she wasn't coming out a door beside the drive-
in gate right this goddamn minute. Wearing white short-shorts.
Rape-me shorts, Rubio called them. When you could see the
bottoms of the ass cheeks. Rubio had a mouth on him. She wore
ratty sneakers. And giant shades. That insect look. Made them all
look like flies. Sexy flies.

She turned around, that ass, that *ass*, and leaned over, pulled a
buggy through the door. No, a stroller. With a baby in it.

Well yeah. That's what you put in strollers.

For a second he was spooked. But just a second. She'd been

skinny when she left home and she was just as skinny now. The thing was small—he squinted at it, pink smush of face surrounded by blankets—but not a newborn. The thing wasn't hers, no way. Course not. Jesus.

So she was a nanny. At seventeen. Rich people had no fucking standards.

She pushed the stroller along the sidewalk. Coming toward him as he cruised. She didn't glance his way. White earbuds in. The wires hung over her tits. Couldn't see the nips. Baggy T-shirt.

He made a U-turn at the corner, followed. Passed her and turned again. She was paying zero attention. Kid could be squalling in its container, she wouldn't have a clue. Probably listening to Lorde. Or Adele. She liked the girly shit. Once he did her with "Hello" playing on her bedside table. Whenever he heard that crap come on he changed the station. Right away.

Plan. Plan. He needed to get inside. Had to get her alone. Four walls. Bed not required. Did he have leverage? What was his leverage now? Always been Rita. But maybe that card had been played out. Was it played out? Might be. Might really be.

He should've thought about this on the drive. Felt too high. The music. Speed. Lights at night. Hadn't thought.

What about this, the nanny job? Could he use that? How?

Ely. Ely and Toff. That was the button to push.

He passed her again, her facing toward him now, and she glanced up. She saw. Stopped walking. Stood there. Stared at him.

He pulled over, parked. Got out. Shit, had to pull up his pants as he slid out. Waist loose. He'd lost weight since she cut out. Which was OK, he could stand to get rid of some flab. But hadn't bothered to wear a belt. The cab-dismount pants-hike, not a good look. Don't think that way. Raw power. Man.

"What are *you* doing here?" she said. Angry. Seemed older behind the sunglasses. Button nose. Lips. Shiny with gloss.

"Came to see you," he said. "What else?"

"Well, you've seen me. Here I am. Now can you go?"

"*See* you," he said. "You know. I missed you."

Sounded desperate. Wished she'd take off the sunglasses. She could be anyone, behind those. He needed to piss. Badly.

"You have to go," she said firmly. "All that stuff's over. You want me to call the cops?"

"Hey!" he said, and his hands went up. She had him on the rails. Not good.

"I will," she said, and slid her phone from a pouch on top of the stroller. "I swear I will. Then what would my mother think?"

"And what about your little family here?" he said. Now he was heating up. "You want them to hear? How Ely and Toff make a buck? You think those rich parents would want a girl from Meth World USA cuddling their rich baby?"

She stared. She raised the hand that didn't hold the phone. Took off the glasses. Wish granted. Her eyes were fierce.

"You're an asshole," she said.

"Newsflash," he said.

They stared at each other.

"One more time," he said. "Last time. It'll be the last. I swear."

"You said that before," she said. "You said it on New Year's. You said it after that Debbie kid's stupid bat mitzvah. You swore it on your mother's grave. When you were shitfaced. Or did you forget? You said, *Just one more time. I swear. On the grave of my sainted mother.* Those exact words."

Showed how drunk he'd been. If his mother was a saint, he was the Dalai Lama.

"But this is different," he said. "You're not here."

She stared some more.

"There. I mean. With me. You live far away now. I know it's over. You moved out."

"Then what are you doing here?"

Throw me a bone. "Lexie. I need it. Just one more time. Then you can—you can take that app off your phone. I won't be able to find you. The—with the GPS."

"So that's how. Fuck. Stupid. Yeah. Sure as shit I'll take it off. Like, instantly. But it won't matter. Because now you know where I fucking *live*."

"You won't be here forever," he said. Weakly. A weak point.

"Forget it," she said. "Just go home, Pete." And turned around. Hit a keypad. Pushed the stroller back through the gate. Closed it with a clang that vibrated. Clang of steel. He heard the lock click. Walked quickly, peered around the tall hedge, through the bars. She was pushing the stroller around the side of the house. Watched her ass as she disappeared.

Trudged back to truck. Tail between legs. Slammed the door. Smacked the wheel with the heel of his hands. Piss-poor showing. Piss-poor. Leaned over, snorted right out of the baggy.

Not giving up. Not yet. She'd come around. He knew his girl. Needed more time. He'd call Rita. One-day delay. Consignment not ready.

Couldn't stay here. What if she did call the cops? Would she? Naw, man. She wouldn't do it. Too risky.

But just maybe.

He started it up, pulled away.

Regroup. Get better sleep.

Skeezy motel. By the time he found it, had to let loose behind a trash can before he even checked in. Then paid cash. Crashed hard on the sagging bed.

When he woke up it was mid-afternoon. Needed a drink, asked at the desk about liquor stores, picked up a bottle of Beam. Drank in the truck. Trying to figure his next move. Finally texted her. *Second thoughts yet?* She texted back *Fuck off.*

Game on, my girl.

Drove back to the motel, showered and shaved. Back in the truck. Drove to the swank pad. Rang the bell at the gate.

Someone Hispanic answered, a woman. "Ee-yes?"

"Here to see Lexie," he said. "She'll know who it is."

The box was silent for a while, then the Hispanic woman came on again.

"She putting down the baby. She see you when the baby sleep."

Better than he expected. He'd figured he might have to wait till the man of the house got back. Throw a scare into her. He didn't give a shit what people thought. Not anymore.

He waited. Made a trip to the truck for some blow and a drink. Came back. Waited again.

Finally. She opened the front door, came down the path in a hurry. Wearing different clothes. A white dress like a sack, with lace at the top and bottom. Closer, he saw she had a chain around her neck with a cross on it. What the fuck.

"They're getting home soon," she said, tense. "You have to go. I mean it."

"I'll go," he said. "If you meet me later."

She looked at him, shaking her head. But she didn't say no.

So he gave her the name of the motel, his room number.

Stopped for a drive-thru burger, went back to the motel.

Stomach unsettled. Took a long shit. Watched part of a game on TV. Showered again. Quickly, he couldn't miss her knock. Was she even coming? She better. Dark outside. The coke was almost gone; he had to save a line for when she got here. He was getting hot. Jerked off so he wouldn't come too fast later. Looked at the bikini photo on his phone. Also popped the blue pill. Not gonna make it easy for her. This was for him. It would last. Cleaned himself up. Drank. Liter bottle half gone.

10:05. 10:43. He was surfing through channels. Faster, faster. Almost like he expected to see her on the screen. Face and tits.

11:14. Knock. Yes. He snorted up the line.

Opened the door. It was a man. Some fat fuck. Shit.

"Phone's down. Girl came to the front desk? She said she wasn't coming to your room. She said to meet her at the truck."

"Yeah, yeah. OK."

Guy stood there, expectant. What did he want, a tip? Fuck that. He shut the door.

Waited for the guy to go away. Then stuffed his keycard in his pocket, was out the door, down to the parking lot. Hands shaking again, dammit. There she was, a bulky hoodie over the white dress. Pink flip-flops. Face lit by her phone. No makeup. Sweet pouty lips. He was already hard.

"Why didn't you text me?" he said, adjusting himself, hand in pocket.

She shrugged, slipped the phone into her hoodie pouch. "I didn't feel like it. And wow. I knew you were cheap. But this place is a shithole. Probably has bedbugs."

"Got rich tastes now, I see," he said.

"Whatever," she said, and shrugged again. "It's in the truck or not at all. And this is the last time. For real. If I ever see you again without my mother right there in the room with us? You're toast. She deserves better anyway. It'd be like ripping off a Band-Aid."

He liked the new Lexiegirl. Assertive. Big girl now. Felt a drop on the end of his dick. Wanted to put it in her mouth. She'd never let him. Threatened to bite. Wouldn't let him kiss her, either. Clamped her mouth shut when he tried. Tight as a nun in the Arctic.

Had he brought the keys to the truck? He hadn't brought the fucking keys.

"Don't leave," he said, and jogged back up to get them. He didn't feel right. Felt strange. Never been this nervous. Booze should've taken the edge off. Had to be the coke. Maybe it was cut with something. Ely didn't do trash coke, most times, but. He hadn't asked how pure it was. Maybe. He fumbled with the keycard.

Then he was back. Didn't even recall being in the room. Had he been there? Like a whirlwind. But the keys were in his hand. She stood there watching him.

"I'll put the seats down," he said. Awkward with the shaking hands. Stop, stop. Thank God for Rubio's king cab, though. His own truck didn't have reclining seats.

She was climbing in the passenger door. Closing it. He shut his own door, reached up to turn the cab light back on. Had to see her.

"What's *wrong* with you?" she asked. "You're sweating."

"Pull your dress up," he said. His teeth were almost chattering. Weird.

"Not taking it off," she said. "Not here."

"Just pull it up, then," he said. Gritted his teeth. "Take off your underwear."

She did. The panties were at her feet. He saw it. Fucking heaven. He couldn't help himself, he reached over and fumbled with her lips. Soft and dry. He felt a sigh come out of him. Lay back and raised his fingers to sniff. Didn't care what she thought of it. He was pressing so hard against his pants it hurt. Fumbled with his button, unzipped the fly. "Get on top of me," he said. They'd never done it like that. That was how he did it with Rita. But here. No room. He couldn't get over there. He couldn't fit himself on top of her. Nothing to brace against . . . he was amped. But also tired. So heavy. His arms felt heavier than lead.

A moment's pause. Would she say no? But then she clambered onto his lap. The steering wheel at her back. Horn honked. "Jesus," she said. "Pete. Seriously. Your color's off. Your face is like, red and gray. You don't look good. Even for you."

"I can still do it," he said. He was a rock. He was huge. "Get on me. Get *on* me."

She tried, but she was dry as bone. *"Ow. Ow."*

"No lube. Sit on my face," he said. "Let me lick you."

She raised herself up, arranged herself. Strong, slender legs. Golden. His face was full of her. Heaven again. He was immersed. But she didn't let it last. Cruel. As soon as she was good to go she took it away and settled down and tried again. She slid down, still there was too much friction at first but she gasped and made it work. He filled her up. He groaned. Was she still on the pill? He'd made her go on the pill at home. Fuck it. Not his business. He didn't care. He didn't give a shit.

She moved up and down.

"Show me your tits," he said. The top of the dress had buttons. She undid them as she moved. Took the tits from the bra. He groaned again and grabbed them, though his arms moved slowly. He squeezed the nipples. They were small and hard. They were perfect.

"Faster," he said. He should be wanting slow, but he didn't. He couldn't. He dropped his arms, watched her tits jiggle. Her face was serious. Not cold, exactly. No, not cold. Not angry, even. Actually her face was kinder than he remembered it being. But serious. Too serious. Mouth closed.

Was she different now? She might be different. He cut off the thought. She was the same. She was the same. She would always be her.

"Show me your tongue," he said.

She opened her mouth a little, let the tip of her tongue rest on her bottom front teeth.

This was it. This was where he always wanted to be. The only place. He wanted to be here for the rest of his life. Just here. Till he disintegrated. Till he was gone to dirt. A single request. People wanted so many things. They had a laundry list. But he only wanted this. Was it so much to ask?

"You're a fucked-up man, Pete," she said. "You're a sad fucking man." Still, not angry. Just matter-of-fact. As she rode him.

"Yeah," he said, half-groan. "I guess so."

She went faster and harder, till she was sweating too. It glowed on her. He gazed up. Sweat dripped into his ear. Tickled. But he ignored it. He didn't need to hear. Only the rush of feeling. His whole body was heavy but his chest was light. He was part of the earth. Mineral. He was the ground and the base. Above him the sun. The most beautiful thing. Maybe she'd come. Was she moaning? Would she come on his cock? Would he receive that gift?

Sunburst. Supernova.

One regret, he thought, after he came. Maybe he was still coming. Because it went on forever. One solitary regret in the long dark hall of this life, only one. Never been in her mouth.

GOD SAVE THE QUEEN

She was freaked out, sobbing. He could barely catch what she was saying. But he got that she was asking him to come over. Like *now*. She didn't say why.

He was wearing the sweats he slept in, didn't bother to change. Took the work truck and drove.

When he got to the house and went in through Lexie's private door, turned out the baby was up and Lexie had her in her room with a bottle. But the baby didn't want it. Lexie was swaying her in her arms, whispering *Shush, Shush*, but the baby was still crying so she laid her down on her bed and wrapped her up in a small blanket. She had a special way of doing it, triangles, really tight.

"There you go, Baby Rae," said Lexie. She always called her

that, never Rachel. Her own idea. He liked it better too. "You're going to be all right. You see?"

Her hair was wet, she must have showered—no makeup, a big T-shirt and cutoffs. Her face was puffy but she had herself under control. Only the baby was crying now.

The child bride didn't normally get up for night feedings, Lexie had said, and the *paterfamilias* never even considered it. That's what an au pair was for.

Lexie swayed the baby some more. Laser focus. He respected it. Baby Rae stopped crying finally and fell asleep. Lexie laid her down on her own bed, got some Kleenex and blew her nose.

"Man, so what's going on?" he asked. He kept his voice down.

She tossed the Kleenex in the trash, opened her mini-fridge and handed him a can of beer. She didn't drink it, but she kept it there for him. A soda for herself. They popped the tabs.

"Let's go outside, OK?" she said.

He nodded and followed her out onto the patio, kept the door open so she could hear if Baby Rae woke up.

"So someone died," she said. "My stepfather."

"Oh, shit," said Jem. "Man. I'm sorry."

She shook her head.

"He's an asshole," she said. "Total. I mean. He was. It's that—I was with him when it happened. Tonight."

"Oh, shit," said Jem. Good line. "That's—"

"I got a couple of hours off, I asked Lora. Because he came down to see me. So I went to meet him, like, where he was staying. This piece-of-shit motel. But then he had a heart attack."

She'd done some CPR, she'd tried, but she'd only even done it on a dummy before. Swim lessons at the Y when she was twelve.

"I called the ambulance. Then they got there and used the shocker things. Paddles."

"Defibrillator," he said. From modern Latin *fibrilla*, diminutive of *fibra*. Fiber.

"Yeah, but it didn't work. So I had to call my mom. It sucked. She like, got totally hysterical."

"Wait. This was happening. And Lora still made you take care of the baby?"

"I mean, I called my mom before I got back. Right from the motel parking lot. I handed the ambulance guys my phone, they told her where they were taking him. I couldn't do much. I don't even remember half of it. She's getting a flight. She's too messed up to drive. But anyway. When I came back I just told Lora she could go to sleep. It's fine."

No, it was bullshit. Child bride should have moved her ass out of the conjugal bed. *Con*, Latin for together. *Jugum*: a yoke. Yoked together. Ox at the plow. The Romans got that right.

She should have picked up her own wailing offspring. Making Lexie stay up all night when this shit just went down? Royal assfuck.

"He was probably on something. He was a drunk and sometimes he did coke. He lived on red meat and pizza. I actually *told* him he looked sick but he ignored me. I *told* him."

"Man. Don't blame yourself. That's just crazy."

She shook her head, drank from her can.

"Seriously," said Jem. "It's not your fault."

He should have brought some pot. She wasn't much of a stoner but if she ever needed to get stoned, it was tonight.

"What am I gonna tell her?" said Lexie. Almost more to herself. "He stopped in to see me. He was supposed to be in Orange

County. That's what she told me on the phone. My mom. She said
he had to pick up some stuff for work, it was delayed. He said. So
I go, yeah, he stopped in to see me. But then. Why was he at that
gross motel? Why was he staying in L.A. at all?"

"I don't get it," said Jem. "Just tell her what happened. Right?"

She glanced at him without really looking, shook her head
again.

"I have to protect her. Like, the way she thinks of him."

"I don't get it," said Jem again. Lexie was kicking at the base
of a metal patio chair with her bare toes. Pretty lightly. But didn't
it hurt?

"He was like, *messing* with me," she said. "OK? Since, like, forever. Well. Two years. It seemed like forever. That's why he was in
town. I bet he didn't even *have* a business trip. Probably told her
some random crap so he could make a run down here. She *can't*
know, Jem. It would turn her whole life to shit."

What was he doing? Was he staring? Adjust his face. Damn.

"Don't *look* at me like that," said Lexie, and stopped kicking. "I
told you he was an asshole. I told you ages ago."

It explained a lot. The online sex for money. Truly fucked.

"I was ready to tell her," she said. "If he didn't leave me alone.
It was always his threat, you know? From the first time. I woke up
in my own bed one night and he was like, *on* me. He said if I told
her it would be worse for her than anyone. How it'd ruin her life.
I thought, he's a pig. For sure. But yeah, he's not wrong, it pretty
much would. Then when I left home I started to think, maybe
she'd be better off. In the end. But now—no way. She can't find
out. Just help me figure it out, Jem. Please?"

And then the guy gets off scot-free. Although yes, dead. So he
would always be scot-free.

"It has to be simple," said Lexie. "Just like, she had a husband, she loved him, he loved her back, and then he had a heart attack and died. That's bad enough. She's not a strong person. She already had a crappy time with my dad. She's like, all about flowers. Kittens and puppies. Well. Not actual kittens and puppies. They don't allow pets in the building. But she likes cute pictures of them."

He finished his beer, crumpled the can. He felt pretty shit. Confused. Brain stuck on her being messed with.

But man. It wasn't about him. Rally.

"Just say he was tired, he wasn't feeling good. Which has to be true, right? Guy had a heart attack. Just say he came up to say hi, he didn't want to drive back to OC tonight, so he was going to crash nearby. It's not incriminating. It'll be fine."

"He wasn't supposed to know where I was. I didn't tell them. But there was this GPS app . . . he got the address off her phone. Admitted it. Which would look weird to her, you know? That he did that."

"So say he called you and you just told him where you were. Being friendly to stepdad. Since he was in the hood."

"OK. But then why was I there? At his motel at *midnight*? Is that a normal time to go see your stepdad at a shitty motel?"

"I guess not. Yeah. Not normal."

She sat down on the half-wall and he sat beside her, bumps on the plaster sticking into his butt. Uncomfortable. He drummed his fingers on his knees.

"Maybe he wanted to come over earlier, say hi and shake hands all around, right? Meet your employers. Check out your new crib. But you had the baby to take care of. And then the baby was sleeping. He had to leave for OC early in the morning. So you said you'd stop by."

"Like, Lora and Paul were out, maybe, and I had to wait till they got back."

"Yeah. That could work. It's still weird, but she'd probably buy it. Right?"

"Shit," said Lexie, and stood up again. "Shit, shit, shit."

"What?"

"His phone. The texts. She could see them."

"Can she get into it?"

"There's got to be a code. But I don't know. Even if there is, maybe she knows it. I don't know!"

"Where is it?"

"I don't know! Maybe in the truck?"

"And the truck. Still at the motel?"

"I guess. I don't know. Yeah. Probably?"

He could do this. He could. She shouldn't have to deal.

"You think the truck's locked up?"

"Jem! I don't *know*. It was like, a blur when I left. They took him away and I just got in my car. Your grandma's car. And *drove*."

"I'll deal, OK? I'll go there. Just give me the name of the motel."

She headed inside, Jem trailing, and called it up on her phone's map app. Seventeen minutes, it said. He typed it into his. When he went out the slider again she was lying down on her side by the sleeping baby, still holding her phone clutched to her chest. Her knees were drawn up. She looked like a baby too.

Drove. Drove. He realized when he was almost there that he hadn't asked about the truck. Hadn't asked her what it looked like. He texted, but no answer. Maybe she'd finally fallen asleep. Damn. Fool's errand.

But when he got to the place, there were only two trucks parked in the lot. The rest were shitty cars. It wasn't the Ritz. One of the trucks had a bashed-in side and Wisconsin plates. Couldn't be that one, right? So he tried the door on the other, a big shiny gray Dodge with a toolbox in the bed. Opened right up.

The driver's seat was laid way back. WTF. Maybe the guy'd been sleeping in it. Shit, keys were here. Anyone could've driven off with the rig. Key ring was lying right on the floor of the driver's seat. He flicked the light on overhead. Looked around for a phone. Felt under the seats. Nothing.

Maybe they'd taken the guy's phone with him. Like, personal effects. But if they bothered with that, why not the keys?

Room. The guy's room. Should have asked her which room he was staying in. Could he ask at the desk? Would they help him? He texted her again, but still nothing.

He sat there for a minute. Then grabbed the keys, turned off the light, got out and pressed the beeper to lock it. Chirp-chirp. Headed for the lobby. It was dark, but there was a doorbell. He pressed it. Heard nothing for a while, so he pressed it again. Starting to feel hopeless. Failed mission, man. Useless.

But then a light went on inside and a guy shuffled toward the door.

"Yeah, sorry," said Jem. He held the truck keys up. Like proof of he was legit. "My stepdad was staying here. He had a heart attack. Can I get into his room, please?"

"Oh, right," said the clerk. Sleepy fat guy. "OK. Yeah. Sorry for your loss. Yeah. Hold on a second."

Zero professionalism. Didn't ask for ID. Not even the stepdad's name, which Jem didn't actually know. Would have been shit out of luck. But the sleepy fat guy didn't have a clue. Lucky.

He came out with a keycard.

"Here you go. 226," he said. "Just leave it in the room."

A rush. Success. Took the cement steps two at a time. Little green light on the lock.

Lights were blazing inside. Messy bed. He saw the phone right away, beside a near-empty bottle of Jim Beam. He almost grabbed the bottle to take a swig. But didn't. Who knew where that guy's mouth had been. Turned the phone on, but got a code prompt. OK. Looked around. Beside the sink there was some ragged-looking shit. A grimy plastic case, razor inside. A bar of soap. The sink had a scum of short hairs on it. Guy'd shaved before he died. Toothbrush, old bristles splayed, yellow and disgusting. Toothpaste. Empty coke-sized Ziploc bag, faint remnants of the powder.

And Viagra.

"Fucking pig," he said. For Lexie.

That was it. No clothes except a dirty T-shirt, wadded on the floor of the bathroom.

He left it all, except the phone and the Viagra. In case the mom came in. She might, right? At some point. Should he keep the truck keys? Yeah. Give 'em to Lexie. He kept the keycard too. You never knew. Took the bottom of his shirt as he went out, wiped the door handle with it. Seen it in shows. Not a crime scene, but still. It should be like he wasn't here. Only the sleepy fat guy had seen him and hadn't asked his name. He could pass for a ghost. The ghost in the machine.

Back at the house, felt satisfied as he went in the slider. Job well done. Lexie was fast asleep. Baby Rae too. He laid the truck keys on the bedside table, placed the phone beside them. Gently. He was stealthy but not stealthy enough.

"Hey," said Lexie, and struggled to sit up. The baby stirred.

"No, no," he whispered. "Go back to sleep. It's OK. I got it."

"No, I'm awake," she said. The baby stopped moving again.

"Phone," he said. "It's locked. And the keys to his truck."

"OK," she said. "Jem. You're the best."

"Text me in the morning," he said. "It's Saturday. I got nothing but time. I'll do whatever. Just text me."

She nodded, settled down again as he went out.

Back at the ranch there were lights blazing. In the kitchen his mother was up, wearing baggy flannel pajamas, waiting for him.

"Where'd you go? It was the middle of the night. It's almost four a.m.!"

"I know, Moms. I'm sorry. It was Lexie. Her stepdad died."

Her face changed, kind of relaxed into sadness.

"Oh, that poor girl."

"He was kind of not a nice guy. But she was there when it happened. His heart. So she's, like, traumatized."

"My God. Of course."

"I'm gonna crash for a couple hours, OK?"

"Yes. Get some sleep, honey."

He lay down on top of the covers. Then a text alert. Plus morning light in the window.

Call me. He hit voice call.

"I got into the phone," said Lexie.

"You did?" Groggy.

"I tried my birthday. No. Then tried some other things. Finally I got an idea and tried another date. My birthday, but the year I turned sixteen. That's when he started—you know. And that was it."

"That's warped." He swung himself out of bed. Where was the bong? He could use a hit.

"It's good I did. There were pictures of me. One in a bikini.

Like, edited so my friends weren't in it. I trashed all of them. And our texts."

"Score," he said.

"Also some photos of this actress. I forget her name. Just like, captured from BuzzFeed or something. She looks kind of like me. I mean, prettier. But."

"Gross."

"You saved my ass."

"Hey. All in a day's work."

"I have to go meet my mother soon. Would you come with?"

Mother. Shit.

"We have to choose an urn. She's going to cremate him."

Urn. Shit.

Clear cue for serious bong use.

Although. The *mater* felt strongly that he should be sober more often. For the sake of his brain. "You're going to need that thing," she said. He'd been working on it. Progress was being made.

Still. Urn for a molester. Plus molester wife and molester victim. That was a challenge, sober.

"I mean, you don't have to. Of course."

"No, no worries. Sure. I'm solid on urns. Done a lot of urn shopping. I can tell a premium urn from a piece-of-shit urn. It's all in the seams. Gotta hold them up to the light. You ladies need my expertise."

She laughed. So good to hear.

He got off the phone, looked it up. Yep, straight Roman. *Urna.* Vessel of baked clay.

Knock. "Jem?"

He opened it.

"You want pancakes?"

"Can they be chocolate-chip?"

"Sure. I think we have some chips."

"OK. Then I have to go to a funeral parlor. They're picking out an urn."

"Oh? Are you sure, honey? It's kind of a family thing. Usually."

"Yeah. She asked me to go."

"Well. As long as her mother's comfortable with it."

He nodded, though he had no idea.

"And don't be stoned for the funeral parlor. Disrespectful."

"Damn, Moms. You read my mind."

"You think people don't know, but they do."

Lexie's stepbrothers cooked meth, a full-on Bryan Cranston scene. The dead molester was a cokehead. Doubtful a whiff of weed would scare off the mom, but his own was a different story.

"Fine, *fine*. I'll just have pancakes. With chips. Hold the Purple Kush. I gotta get dressed."

She smiled and closed his door.

Since he agreed to go to private school next year she'd eased way up on him. She thought it would be a magic bullet. He'd be Ivy League–bound in no time flat. He didn't want to disillusion her, but he feared the day reality set in. For her, not him. The place would surely suck ass.

However. *Audentes fortuna iuvat.* Fortune favors the bold. Some Virgil shit right there.

He put on *Anarchy in the U.K.* Loud. One good thing about the middle-class Los Feliz digs: the neighbors were too nice to yell about loud music in the daytime. Or too poor. Not poor, get real, even this modest casita was a million five, but not as rich. In his old hood, the neighbors used to send over the help to ask him to turn the music down. Which really bit, because when the help asked, some under-minimum-wage lady from Honduras with a hangdog look, it was way harder to say no.

Picked out some somber-looking duds. Passed over the T-shirt that said FUCK OFF YOU FUCKING FUCK. Respect. Theme of the day.

After the pancakes he felt like going back to bed, but pushed himself into the truck, pulled up the funeral parlor on Google Maps. Listened to Sid as he drove. *She ain't no human being.* Same queen, man. Over there in England it was still the same queen it had always been. She outlasted Sid. She outlasted them all. That queen refused to die.

The funeral place was a bummer. Not exactly upscale. This was where losers went when they died. Razor wire across the empty lot next door. Weeds in the sidewalk cracks. Lexie and her mother weren't here yet. She texted they were on their way. Shit if he would cross the threshold without them. He sat in the truck. The neighborhood was blighted. Homeless guy across the street, sitting against the boarded-up window of a shut-down bakery, was actually messing with his works. In broad daylight.

Wanted to say, Hit the methadone clinic, man. That shit is *free*.

Die rich, was the lesson here.

Almost enough to make you *want* to go Ivy League.

There was the Dodge truck from last night, pulling up to the curb. Lexie was at the wheel. Parked and a lady got out the passenger side, skinny and wretched, with long pink fingernails and a little beige purse hanging off one shoulder. She didn't look like Lexie at all.

Man, did he wish he was stoned. Got out of his own truck anyway. Into battle. *Ubi mors ibi spes.* Where there is death there is hope.

"My friend Jem," said Lexie. "He's been a big help. Jem, this is my mom. Rita."

The mother lady nodded. Big bags under her eyes. Altered state. Maybe not drugs, maybe tiredness. But altered state either way. Seemed barely there. Jem put out his hand for a shake, but she just grabbed it sideways for a second, then dropped it.

Inside it was like funeral parlors on TV, different coffins on display. Except grimier. Nothing looked new. The flowers were all fake. Bad lighting. Those ceilings with pockmarks in them, low and white. A guy came forward. Short. Gayish. Maybe Latino, maybe Asian. Hard to peg.

"We'd like to see the urns, please," said Lexie. Rita just stood there, fiddling with her purse. Unzipped it, took out a tissue from a travel pack.

The short guy led them back past the coffins to a shelf of urns. Not a big talker. Not much of a salesman. No wonder the place was decrepit.

"Price list," he said, and handed them a binder. The vinyl was fingertip-smeared. Brown-red. Maybe ketchup. Jesus. Or barbecue sauce. Really?

"You know," said Jem, aside to Lexie while her mother stood staring at a green pot, "we can go somewhere else. I mean, there are other places. Even on a budget. I can look that shit up."

"She picked this one," said Lexie. "First she was going to get a Ball jar from Target. I said, let's get a real urn. I think she liked the name of the place. It's no big deal. Don't worry."

Rita was still just standing there. She was shivering, he noticed. One thing the place did have: powerful AC. It was frigid as a meat locker.

What *was* the name? He hadn't noticed.

Lexie stood with her mother, put an arm around her waist.

"How about that one?" she said, and pointed to a plain gray thing. "He would've been down with that. Kind of industrial. Like, masculine."

"OK," quavered her mother, "fine," so Jem told the short guy, who was standing there doing something on his phone. He nodded, went to the back and came out with a box. Lexie got Rita's wallet, paid with her credit card.

When they left, Jem looked up at the front. It said WING ON FUNERAL PARLOR.

Then they were standing beside the big Dodge. Rita was looking at the sidewalk, dabbing at her eyes with the Kleenex. Lexie held the box in one hand, got the keys from her hoodie pocket with the other.

"You guys eat anything?" asked Jem. "Could I take you to lunch?"

He had zero appetite. But what else was there to offer?

"We didn't eat," said Lexie. "Mom. You hungry?"

Rita shook her head.

"I am," said Lexie. "I'm actually starving."

Then again, restaurant, wretched crying lady . . . bad scene.

"How about this," said Jem. "We'll go back to my place."

WTF. Had he said that?

His moms, though. Maybe she could do something. Maybe she could talk to the lady.

"Then if you do get hungry, my mom can fix you something," he said. "If not, you can kick back. There's guestrooms. You could rest a bit, Mrs.—Rita."

Rita didn't say anything. Either nodding or shaking her head. Couldn't tell.

"I like it," said Lexie.

"OK. You just follow me there."

He texted before he started the truck. Had to give the moms a heads-up. She was welcoming, but she liked to tidy the house if people were coming. Though it was always tidy. Outside his room.

She'd been watching for them when they pulled up, because she opened the door as they were coming in from the drive. She had a serious expression, but also brought a smile. Concerned but friendly. She was good that way. The moms was hella appropriate.

"Lexie," she said, and held both of Lexie's hands in hers. Smile gone. "And this must be your mother. I'm so sorry for your loss."

"Rita," said Rita, and then burst into full-out tears. Wailing, almost. Mascara was all around her eyes. Nose running. Straight embarrassing.

The moms steered her inside. Jem and Lexie followed. Kind of a lame feeling. "Why don't you get Rita a glass of ice water, Jem," and so he and Lexie veered off toward the kitchen.

"Can we let your mom deal a bit?" said Lexie. "Rita keeps doing this. I don't know how to make it stop."

"Yeah, no."

They hung in the kitchen a few minutes, Lexie not wanting to get back in the fray. He rustled up a bag of chips, which she ate like she hadn't eaten in days. Salt and vinegar. Then got them sodas, poured the glass of water.

"I'll take it in," he said.

"Thank you."

So he trudged back to the living room, where the two moms sat on a couch, his mother patting Rita's knee. Rita was talking between sniffs. Hard to catch the words.

"I just can't believe it," she said. "It's not—I can't believe it."

Rita didn't seem to notice him with the water, but his mother looked up and reached for it.

"Here," she said to Rita. "Drink a little. You need to rehydrate."

"He's—he was such a good man," said Rita.

Golden.

"I'm sure he was," said the moms. If only she knew.

Once he would've wanted to say to the mom, stop blubbering. He fucked with your daughter.

But now. No. Didn't want to. At all.

"They made me . . . I had to look at his . . ."

The crying started again. He took it as his cue. Found Lexie still standing in the kitchen. A trapped animal.

"Can we smoke some weed?"

He could get her stoned, sure, and not even partake, but the moms would suss it out and maybe get pissed. No. Surely get pissed.

"Normally yeah. Of course. But she asked me not to, today. Out of respect. Which I think would include you."

"Yeah. I get it," said Lexie.

She looked forlorn, standing there with her Coke.

"You want to listen to some tunes? Just hide out in my room?"

She fished for her phone.

"We have an appointment at the crematorium," she said. "But not for a couple hours."

Were they going to watch him burn? Stand there beside the furnace? People did that. Occasionally. He read it somewhere. But no, probably not. Don't ask.

"Can we go outside?" said Lexie. "The backyard. Fresh air."

So they went out. There were trees. Flowers. Purple and white and orange. Grass yellow from the water restrictions.

"A crazy lady owned this house before," he said. "She thought there were midgets living in the attic, I guess. Like seven. She thought she was Snow White. Or that's how Nina tells it."

"Midgets? Or dwarves?" said Lexie, walking, swinging an arm to trail one hand along the bushes. "They're different. Right?"

"How Nina tells it, at first she thought they were little, but then they turned big. So then she had to sell. She was OK with them living there when they were small."

"I could see that. If Pete was a dwarf, he might have been easier to deal with."

"You think?"

"Well. Maybe."

"Yeah. You're being, like, a heightist."

"Is that a thing?"

"For sure. Listen. And get this straight. A dwarf can molest just as good as a tall guy. Any day of the week."

She chortled. Score.

"Molestation ability, it's not all in the legs. Am I right?"

"You're right, Jem."

"Upper body strength. That's more of a factor."

"A dwarf could have great upper-body strength."

"That guy from *GoT*? Peter whatever? I bet he has fair upper-body strength."

"Dinklage. Peter Dinklage."

"Man. It's not enough the guy has to be a dwarf, he also has to have the last name *Dinklage*."

"Jem?"

They both turned. Moms at the back door. She walked out to them.

"Your mother's lying down, Lexie. I gave her a Klonopin."

"Word," said Jem. "Can I get one of them?"

"Thank you," said Lexie. "Thank you *a lot*. For all the help."

"Now. Would you like a cheese sandwich? Or I also have some gazpacho."

He left the two of them once they got into the house, headed to the downstairs bathroom. Rita'd left her purse on the sink. Gaping open, the top of a pack of Menthols sticking out. Even if she wasn't messy and crying, he'd feel sorry for her. That scarecrow body, and her gray roots showing up patchy on her head. And then the long nails. Fake. Hot pink.

He was an asshole. It was poverty. He got that. What did she do for work? Lexie had told him but he couldn't remember. Maybe answering phones somewhere. Yeah, that was it. At a locksmith or something. Been doing it forever.

Lexie wouldn't end up like that. No fucking way. He wouldn't let it happen.

Course, Lexie could look after herself.

But still.

Pissing, he looked at the purse again. It was a dirty beige, maybe fake leather. Vinyl or whatever. It had a little fringe. Some of the pieces of the fringe were missing and the paint on the zipper was half peeled off. It had been used a lot.

Lexie had been used. Sometimes a picture came into his head—only a half-picture. A hint of a picture. The heart attack. Had that been during—? Had Lexie let him—? Shit. *Let* was a fucked-up word. Guys died like that. Old guys. Died in the sack. Plugging away. Maybe it happened more often with Viagra. Was that true? Nah, there'd be too many big lawsuits. Right? So glad he hadn't met the guy. Couldn't fill in the blanks. Never wanted to see a photo of him. If someone tried to show him one, man. He'd turn his face away so fast.

She'd been used, and now she thought of her mother. She only wanted to protect her mother. Her mother who, fuck knew, should have protected *her*. But Rita. You only had to meet her once to know she couldn't protect jack shit.

Did he respect it? No. He didn't respect it.

Didn't matter. It just was.

He picked up the bag, poked the cigarette pack farther in so it wouldn't fall out, and left the bathroom.

Met Rita in the hallway, bumbling out of the guestroom. Bleary and half-asleep. Mouth rubbery. Maybe she'd taken a pill.

"That's mine!" she said. Grabbed for the purse.

"You left it in the bathroom. I was bringing—"

"It's mine!"

Like anyone else would want the ratty thing.

"Right, I was just—"

"You can't take it!"

Then she was slipping through the guestroom door again, hunched over the bag, hugging it. The door slammed in his face.

He stood there. Had he done something wrong? Apparently. Maybe he shouldn't have touched it. Not his business.

Whatever.

Went into the dining room, where Lexie and his moms were eating. Sat down with them, though he wasn't hungry.

"This is good," said Lexie to the moms.

He had a flashback to the divorce: moms crying, ragged. Now her face shone. She was almost serene. Even spooning up soup, she looked elegant. Back then he'd been like Lexie was now. Wanting to help. Trying to shelter. Something like that.

Then Rita was there. She held her purse still and was shaking.

"He tried to take my bag," she said, nodding her head at him.

"Pardon?"

"He tried to take my bag," repeated Rita.

"I found it on the bathroom sink," he protested. "Was bringing it out. In case she forgot where she left it."

"I didn't forget!"

"OK, OK," he said, and raised his hands. Surrender. Lady was totally wigging.

"He's taking my things!"

"Mom," said Lexie. "No one's stealing from you. OK?"

It was pretty ridiculous, the idea. Rita stood there all sticklike and messy, her face a contortion. Jem felt the hairs stand up on his neck, the backs of his hands. Weird how your flesh could crawl even when you hadn't done much. Guilty over nothing.

"I'm sure he didn't mean to overstep," said the moms. But she looked at Jem sternly.

"I'm really sorry," he said to Rita. "Just trying to help. Kind of like, keep stuff tidy. You know?"

"You can't take other people's things!" said Rita.

Something was weird in her face. Something was off. Like someone had slapped her. Like she had a mask on. And it didn't fit right.

"You can't just take things from people," she said. "You can't just—you can't do that. You can't go in and *take* them. And wreck them! You can't take what's not yours!"

That was when he saw. That was it. Why her mouth was all twisted, her eyes crazy.

It was because she knew. She knew about the dead husband. She knew exactly what he'd been doing.

Maybe she'd known for a long time. Known and never said a word. Because she was so desperate to keep him. Keep everything the same. Her life. She was so desperate.

It was just true.

He'd never been so sure of anything.

But Lexie. He glanced at her. Lexie had no idea.

Then looked at Rita again. She met his eyes. Locked in.

He was right.

He felt a wave of sickness. Almost dizzy. Blinked slowly. The dizziness receded.

Lexie hadn't picked up on any of it.

She put down her sandwich and got up.

"Hey, Mom," she said gently, and slipped an arm around her mother's shoulders. "It's gonna be all right. You're just in shock. Maybe come lie down again. OK?"

Then she steered her out of the room.

She had no idea her mother knew.

She wouldn't have believed it.

And she would never know. She *would not know*. Not from him.

Cadavera vero innumera. Truly countless bodies, was what it meant. People got caught in their own wars all the time. You never knew what wars they could be fighting. No idea. But when you could, you dragged them off the battlefield.

Some were heavier than others. Harder to move. Some were lighter. Some were dead already and others were only dying, but none would ever be the same.

THOSE ARE PEARLS

Marnie was married now, and with the marriage had come peace.

Her husband was a dim man. Not in the sense that he wasn't smart—he was smart enough to make a lot of money—but in the sense that he often went unnoticed, as though the light avoided him. He could stand in a room and hardly be seen.

Still, his presence was pleasant. It had a tranquilizing effect. If you were tired, his conversation could lull you to sleep. Not a bad quality. He was like Ambien.

Marnie was less angry. The money was part of it. They had a big house in Austin, in a rich neighborhood near a river that was really a lake. Or a lake that was really a river. Endangered lizards lived in it. "No, salamanders," corrected Marnie, when Nina said lizards. "Water, get it? Lizards don't like water. Lizards like sand. Or jungles. These ones like *water*."

Nina remembered something about lizards that lived in the ocean—huge ones with spikes on their back. Iguanas, maybe. But she didn't want to argue with her sister. Marnie would say: "Why are you so invested in being right? Do you *need* to be right?"

Not really, Nina wanted to answer. But I *may* be right, now and then. It's not *impossible*. Technically.

They took her out on a boat. The salamanders were so rare you never saw them. Unless you went to a small museum in a certain park, where some were on display in a tank. Even there, they hid behind the plastic plants. Maybe they weren't rare after all. Maybe they were just shy. You could see other animals from the boat, though—turtles with moss on their shells, swimming or sitting on tree branches. Ospreys and great blue herons perched on the banks.

Lewis paddled while she and Marnie talked. Marnie, mostly. Marnie talked about decorators and taxes and vacations. They were going to the Caymans soon. They would stay in a resort where there were flowers on the pillows. Or maybe not whole flowers, maybe just rose petals. A second honeymoon, said Marnie.

During the first she'd gotten a urinary tract infection.

"Do-over," said Lewis, flipping his paddle.

Later Lewis went into the office—he worked weekends, often—and Marnie got out the wine. She wanted to have children, she said, but Lewis wasn't sure. It was the one thing that they disagreed on.

Nina thought, Well, it's not exactly a *minor* point, but she just nodded and listened, sipping the wine.

"He likes kids fine," said Marnie. "And he thinks I'd be a good mother, of course."

"OK," said Nina. "So . . . ?"

"It's, like, the *world*," said Marnie, and shrugged.

"The world?"

"He says he doesn't want to bring them *into* it," said Marnie. "You wouldn't think it, because he's such a sweet guy, right? But at times he can be negative."

They'd met at a self-help seminar in a hotel conference room, the same series Marnie had insisted Nina sign up for. Though Marnie didn't call it self-help. She said it was *language technology*. There, Marnie said, Lewis had seemed so positive. Embracing possibility. But later, after they started dating, it turned out he only embraced some possibilities. Not all of them.

"The possibility of kids, he isn't enrolled," said Marnie. "It wasn't a total deal-breaker for me. So I said yes when he proposed. But I was kind of thinking, if I got pregnant by accident, he wouldn't make me get an abortion. I mean, he grew up Catholic. But he's so careful? It'll never happen. Condoms! I mean what married guy insists on condoms? But he does. It's like he doesn't trust me with the pill!"

And rightly not, apparently.

"So what is it about the um, world?" asked Nina.

"Like, everything."

Nina waited.

"God, I don't know. Global warming? At work he has to research crops. And insurance. He talks about the future like it's not going to be normal. At *all*. I kind of tune it out. It starts to sound paranoid, you know? Next he'll be stockpiling canned foods in the basement."

Marnie never asked her about Lynn. She knew how he'd died, and when Nina said *motorcycle accident* she said she was sorry. But then she said motorcycles were deathtraps. You took your life in your hands when you rode one, she said. It came so close to blaming Lynn that Nina had felt a gate shut inside her, even her face closing. She'd changed the subject back to Marnie. Safer.

"I'm hoping it'll pass," said Marnie. "We still have a few years. If we do some more seminars, maybe he'll start to feel more positive. Get enrolled."

Nina smiled, reassuring, she hoped. Reached for an olive.

"But you, I mean, you're three years older than me," said Marnie. "If you want a kid you should get cracking, right? You could go to a sperm bank. Have you thought of that?"

Then she talked about her upcoming vacation again. Lewis had booked a suite, and couples massages.

The guestroom had a queen bed and, on end tables and shelves, several photos of Marnie and Lewis. Shots of them doing leisure activities and looking pleased. In one they held ski poles and wore woolen hats with snowflakes gathered on them, smiling and leaning their heads together. (Aspen, Marnie had said when she first showed her in.) In another they were on a beach, also smiling. Somewhat tanned. Winter and summer. Two seasons of happiness were shown.

When couples came to stay, when they lay in the bed, did they feel Marnie and Lewis were happily watching them?

She wondered if people in the Caymans also kept pictures of themselves throughout their homes, themselves watching their guests. And watching *them*. Themselves, looking on happily as they lived. Reminding them to be happy, maybe. You've done it before. You can do it again!

No one kept sad photos on the walls, or photos of themselves feeling harassed while buying groceries.

Did people in Africa put self-portraits in their guestrooms? People in Azerbaijan? She'd never kept pictures of herself on her walls and shelves, but many of her sellers did. It was common.

She couldn't sleep—too bad Lewis wasn't around—so she got up and browsed the bookshelves. Display volumes of Shakespeare, all perfect and likely never opened, with gold titles stamped on them. "THE TEMPEST." She cracked it open.

Full fathom five thy father lies;
Of his bones are coral made;
Those are pearls that were his eyes.

Alone. Crying. Dammit. She hadn't done this in months.
Full fathom five his father lies.
The words pulsed in her head like a tide.

Lynn had been the love she chose. That chosen love saved you from the mandatory kind. The ones you *had* to love. It made the burden of that mandatory love feel light.

Without it the duty weighed more.

In the morning she was eager to go, her bag neatly packed. She'd packed it fastidiously, so as to spend more time alone in her room. Marnie drove her to the airport. She said she didn't know when she'd be in L.A. next. "Well, you're always welcome," said Nina.

A white lie. But Marnie wouldn't call her bluff.

And Marnie wasn't her sister, she thought, rolling her bag through the doors to the terminal. Not really. That woman used to be her sister. Long ago.

She texted Ry after the plane landed, when it was still taxiing. He was the only one who understood. He'd sent her links to songs Lynn liked, songs he and Lynn had played together. Drum and bass. Sometimes they'd made their own arrangements. Or sometimes he just texted one word, *Missing*.

Let's get a drink, she typed.

Sure, he typed back.

On the curb at LAX she waited for her ride staring at the white spaceship. The flying saucer, futuristic. She'd never known what purpose it served but she'd always liked it. Someone had said there was a restaurant there, or once had been. At first the restaurant had rotated, many years ago, but no longer.

People passed with their suitcases. Some backpackers, muscular and healthy, speaking another language. Swedish? Or Norwegian. Then a monk. Orange robes. He lit up a cigarette. Was that even allowed? Could you still smoke, once enlightened?

Maybe you smoked even more.

What *was* enlightenment? Insight, she'd read. Deep understanding. Freedom from desire. Sure, that made sense. But desire for cigarettes, wouldn't that count? Easier said than done, obviously. Maybe he was a beginner monk. Though he looked pretty old.

But say you succeeded and erased desire. Say you had no cravings and no petty self-interest, but only a feeling of humility. Surpassing peace. She'd read that too. *Surpassing peace.*

What then?

If you weren't a monk, but still overwhelmed by that humility, how did you spend your days?

Maybe you could devote yourself to service. Show up at a soup kitchen or a homeless shelter, work for free. Would they let you?

And what about rent, what about not becoming homeless your-self? How did you work for free? And also still have enough to eat?

Life wasn't set up for surpassing peace.

She dropped her bag at home and got in the car, drove to meet Ry at a bar on Sunset. It was a dive bar, old and dim. Ry didn't like bright light. He hated it. He had to be under bright lights onstage—he'd gotten used to it, he said. He shrank into his instru-ment and disappeared. But in regular life there was no instrument, so he had to stay tucked away. They sat at a dark corner table.

She told him about the trip to Austin, about Marnie and Lewis. In the end, she didn't have much to say about it. Except for the turtles. And the birds. The salamanders that hid.

Ry nodded. He didn't say much either.

He had a talent for sympathy.

A drunk guy blundered up to them. It was a bar that had a lot of regulars—day drinkers, unshaven.

"Let's have Christ for president," sang the drunkard along with the jukebox.

"Fat chance," said a woman on a barstool.

"Spot me a beer," he said to Ry. "It's what Jesus would do."

Ry hesitated a moment, then took out a five and handed it over.

"Happy hour," he told Nina. "The PBRs are four bucks."

"You're the risen messiah," said the drunkard, and swayed his way back to the bar.

"Been waiting a long time to hear that," said Ry.

But after a few minutes another drunk guy came over, younger and with a shaved head.

"Heard you're giving out beers," he said.

Ry looked at him, then at Nina.

"I gave out *one*," he said.

"If one, why not two?"

"Oh for Chrissake," said Ry.

By the time they left he'd paid for three more drinks and all his cash was gone. The man he gave his last bills to—four ones, all that were in his wallet—was irritated. He took them, but shook his head and muttered something they couldn't hear.

"Maybe he expected you to offer your credit card," said Nina, on the pavement.

"Break out the plastic," said Ryan.

"Give an inch, they'll take a mile."

"I wasn't trying to impress you. I'm just bad at saying no."

"Hey," she said, and jostled him with her elbow. "I was already impressed."

In his face she thought she saw a flash of hidden feeling— regret or embarrassment. As though he might be saying to him-self: *Remember, we're just friends.*

Or maybe she was flattering herself.

Anyway, it didn't really matter. Because they were.

Driving down Crescent Heights she thought about taking a shower. She'd take a shower as soon as she got in the front door. Good to be back in L.A. Her car and her city.

Lights, red and blue, flashed in the rearview mirror.

Shit! Shit. How long had it been behind her? How many drinks had she had? She couldn't remember. Even two could put you over the limit. Her shoulders tightened as she turned into the side street. Breathing was fast. They could suspend your license. Arrest you, even. Couldn't they? Lynn had been patted down once. The cop had kicked his feet apart, like on TV. Bound his hands with a plastic tie. He'd been sober and driving six miles over the speed limit.

Did she have her registration? Insurance? It was on her phone, the insurance. An app. Her phone was almost out of juice, the charger still packed away. Her suitcase in the trunk. Fumbling in her bag in the passenger seat, in her wallet . . . she flicked on the overhead.

A flashlight. She rolled down the window quickly. Couldn't see his face.

"License and registration, please."

She got them out of her wallet, fingers shaking. "My insurance is current, but I'd have to pull up the app and maybe download—something—"

Babbling. Police always made her nervous. Even before Lynn's stories. Did the policeman hear her? She tapped on the app. *Password*. What was it? Oh. The usual. She used the same password for everything. *View Your ID Cards*.

Would he ask her to walk a straight line? Touch the tip of her nose?

"Do you know why I stopped you, miss?"

"No, I'm sorry. I'm really not sure."

"You can't tell me what you did back there?"

She tried to cast herself back, but it was a blank. She'd been driving, was all. Wanting to take a shower.

She looked at him. Sharp nose, small eyes.

"I don't know, Officer."

Lynn said to always call them *officer*. They needed to dominate.

"Have you had anything to drink tonight?"

He asked her right out. Just like that. And the car hadn't even been weaving!

Did she have to answer?

There was a shout and he turned away to look behind him.

Across the street, on a lawn, two men were in a huddle. She tried to make out what they were doing, but it was too dim. There were street lights and porch lights but trees too, and the men were tossing around beneath one, in a pit of shadow. One of them was yelling.

The policeman crossed the street, flashlight out, breaking into a jog.

She could just drive. Pull away from the curb, screeching. A fugitive! The cruiser giving chase. Chaos!

He hopped over the curb and onto the grass, the spot of his flashlight bouncing. Then the men were running, and he was running. All three of them ran around the side of the house.

Disappeared.

She sat waiting. She was alert.

A gunshot might sound. Or a cry.

But there was no gunshot.

Other cars passed her open window, stopped at the light ahead. One had a thumping bass that made her head hurt. Subwoofers, Lynn had said. So obnoxious. She tapped her phone lightly on the steering wheel and sat staring at the red light, impatient for the car with the bass to drive off.

She couldn't drive off, though.

She turned on the radio.

If the policeman came back, he might make her get out of the car. Might kick her feet apart and cuff her hands with a plastic tie. At least then she'd be echoing Lynn. Doing what Lynn had done, or what had been done to him.

Her life could be lived as an echo, her movements organized to imitate his. Take what she knew of his history and live in it herself. A playback, a ripple. A phantom of him.

The real ghosts were the ones that lived under your skin.

Still no one came back. From the row of houses, the shadows of the trees, there was nothing.

Should she just go?

Twenty minutes had passed. Maybe more.

She almost stepped on the gas. Her foot rested there. But then—she wasn't that drunk. She didn't feel drunk at all. She would stay. She'd be OK.

She opened her door and got out, walked back to the cruiser. Raised her phone and snapped a picture of the plates. Called it in.

The policeman had pulled her over for a traffic violation, she told the dispatch woman. But now he was gone.

Dispatch said thank you, then told her to stay where she was.

More waiting. That was the reward for the dutiful phone call. She leaned against the side of her car.

But she felt restless.

When there was a lull in traffic she crossed the road, walked in the dip of shade under the trees. Along the side of the house, where there was a green, curled-up hose and garbage cans, she heard something. A cat? Something crying, maybe.

Behind the house was an alley. An orange tree hung over it, or maybe lemon. Some rotten ones on the ground.

Lying beyond them, near a curl of old carpet against a low wall, was a man. The policeman. She ran over, bent down.

He lay on his back, one of his arms and his head shaking. His eyes were open, but he didn't turn his head to look at her.

"I called them! They're coming," she said.

She couldn't see what was wrong with him.

Maybe he nodded, or maybe it was the shaking.

"Can you tell me what happened?" she asked.

She looked at his torso, his legs. Was there an injury? A hole in him? She couldn't tell. Should she touch his shirt?

"Did someone shoot you?"

He moved his head back and forth. Looked like no. And she hadn't heard a shot, but she couldn't be sure. Beneath his back there could be blood pooling.

He mumbled something, or tried to. *Medicine?*

She asked him if he meant he was sick. Did he have medicine on him? Medicine she should give him?

But he was fading.

She'd call again and tell them he was in the alley. But she'd left her phone in the car. Hadn't brought it. Thoughtless. She'd have to leave him here to make the call.

When he'd stood at her car window, looming, his nose had been sharp and his eyes small. Now they weren't sharp, weren't small as he lay there. Just a man's face. The eyes were closing. He could be falling asleep, could be dreaming.

He had a gun at his waist. Also resting.

She was useless. She had to go make the call and bring the others. Tell them to send an ambulance.

Still, kneeling beside him she could barely make herself get up and walk.

She'd met Lynn this way—over a man stretched out on the ground, a man who was hurt. The day his friend had almost drowned. She'd had to call the paramedics then too.

Maybe that was when affection crept in. When it seeped in, unexpected. At least, for her. It wasn't just sympathy. It was more.

Was it just her this happened to? Or was it this way for all of them? That when they fell they could be loved?

Love came when they laid their bodies down.

OH CHILD OF EARTH

It wasn't the lawsuit that prompted her decision, the lawsuit Paul decided to bring against the deaf guy in the beat-up Hyundai who put a two-inch ding on his BMW and didn't have enough insurance to cover the paint job at his overpriced body shop. It wasn't the time he scrolled through apparently comical images on his phone, chuckling and shaking his head ruefully, while Lora was crying next to him in the kitchen. (She saw that one from a position behind him as she stood leaning on the walker, her jaw dropped in amazement.) Or even the time she heard him say to Lora, before God and everyone, including his own son, *Your tits look droopy in that bra.* Sober as a judge when he said it. Not that drunkenness would be an excuse either. He would never have pulled that with his first wife.

It was not any of these incidents, nor many others she'd witnessed. Although they were all neat demonstrations of her son's poor character. Moral and otherwise.

No, it was simply the realization that he didn't need her money, didn't need anything from her anymore, but others did. There were others in need.

So she made an appointment with the estate lawyer and had Lexie drive her there. She wasn't wealthy by Paul's standards, of course, but her dear old house had sold well enough. She wanted the money from it to mean something.

The lawyer's office was in Century City, whose verticality she used to feel was so out of place. Las Vegas without the lights or casinos. Lexie went off on a grocery run after getting her situated in his waiting room. A woman on the sofa opposite, legs crossed and expensive bag nestled beside her like a small, curled-up dog, was talking on her cell. "First he said Muslims were the worst customers. But then suddenly he started going on about Indians. Yeah. From India. Right, there's crossover. So he like, zeroed in. From Muslims to Indians. *Indians* are the worst, he said. He goes, there was this one Indian? He was such a tool! The other customers were in *shock*, he said, as they witnessed this Indian guy's behavior. He said, you could feel their ideas about Indians . . . just *expanding*."

Then the lawyer's receptionist called her in, and there was the usual struggle to get up. She had to let the receptionist help.

She wouldn't mention the changed will, of course. Didn't want anyone to feel beholden. She'd laid her plans, that was all. Half the funds would go to Jem and Baby Rae in case Paul went bankrupt and couldn't provide for her grandchildren: a fool and his money, etc. The rest would go to Lexie. She'd written a note to Paul explaining her logic. So that he wouldn't take it as a personal affront.

He *would* take it that way, of course, despite the note, but she had done her best. And he'd get over it. It was pennies to him. Chump change.

She didn't plan to die yet, not while she could still read and write, but she was well prepared. The trick would be to choose her moment. After her usefulness was gone, before the onset of Alzheimer's or dementia. Whichever card she was dealt. A narrow window, possibly. Could be easy to miss.

Well, that was always the trick. And no second chances.

Her people were decent planners as a rule, the people of the book. Of course she was fully assimilated: the missionaries hadn't even known she was a Jew, or not till long after the war, at least. She only found out herself when she was eight. A faux WASP. A WASP by the grace of Stalin. She liked to think her war-orphan upbringing might justify some leniency from Yahweh over the defection, should he be proven, quite surprisingly, to exist. Other Jews wouldn't forgive her, that was true. But he might.

Had she been a better parent than her parents would have been, had they lived? The evidence was against it. She'd gone through her old photos yesterday and thrown out some, but kept the faded sepia-toned print she had from their wedding day. Vilnius. Her father had died in Siberia at Kolyma Gulag, likely frozen, while her mother and sister had fetched up at the other end of Soviet space and probably starved to death. She had a picture of the sign at the front gate of the camp where they'd disappeared. Translated, it read: AKMOLA LABOR CAMP FOR WIVES OF TRAITORS TO THE MOTHERLAND.

She'd been dreamy that day, felt almost nostalgic as she picked through the folder of old photos, her own wedding, Paul as a baby and then as a boy. She gave those all to Lora, who exclaimed over them. How cute! She'd have them scanned right away! Order a special album!

Turning back to her screen, she bit into a cracker and skimmed a new Levada poll on current perceptions of Stalin. *54% of Russians now believe he was a wise leader who led the nation to prosperity,* it said.

The cracker turned to sawdust in her mouth.

She sat there for a minute. Helpless.

Then picked up her cell, called Lora to come back.

"Oh, sure. But can I do my nails while we talk? I know you don't like the smell. But the salon was all booked today. I couldn't get in. And they look *terrible.*"

"Of course, dear. Yes."

So Lora came in, tottering on some glittery high-heeled sandals that seemed to have liquid floating in the platforms, and opened a window. She slipped off the sandals and took out bottles from a kit she carried, various bits of plastic. Arrayed them on the coffee table.

"What are those?"

"Oh! It's so sweet you don't know! Toe separators. See? You put them on like this."

She slid the foam mold between her toes.

"Haven't you ever gotten a pedicure?"

"I have not," said Aleska.

"You should go with me next time!"

"Surely I'm too old to start. I wouldn't want a stranger having to touch my crone's feet."

"It's fun! They do like, calf massages. Exfoliation! You should totally go with me!"

Exfoliation. Jesus. The child bride, as Jem used to call her, was ignorant of aged bodies. Her skin was paper-thin. It would peel off in strips.

"The truth is, I wanted to ask you something."

"Shoot!"

She plied a cotton ball, dabbing at the toenails. Bright red on the cotton like blood on snow.

"First, dear, I don't know if I've thanked you enough. For letting me live in this guesthouse."

"Oh my gosh! Of course. It's actually great. Is everything OK? It's not too small?"

"It's perfect. And I know it was all you."

"No, I mean—Paul wanted it too."

"Mmm. But you pushed for it, didn't you?"

"I—he was—he was completely on board."

Meaning he had not been.

"Anyway. I'm deeply grateful. It's far, far better than some group-living arrangement. It's a lovely place to finish up my life."

"Finish—but that's so dark! *Aleska!*"

"Not dark, dear." She almost laughed, but kept her face serious. "Just realistic. Old people die. And Lexie's been doing a wonderful job, hasn't she?"

"She's *amazing*. She's so great with Baby Rae? I'm, like, amazed."

Even the mother called her baby by Lexie's name for her.

"She can get her to stop crying in a minute. And I never would have pumped this long if Lexie didn't encourage me. She read, like, an article by a doctor? It said it made the baby healthier. Like, their immune system. I'm gonna do six months. I promised her. I mean, Paul isn't that into it. And it does feel weird, like you're a cow being milked."

"It's just like that, isn't it."

"Yeah. It totally is. Paul wants me to switch to formula like *now*. He said he wants them all to himself. But I said, six months."

She had to repress a shudder.

"Very good. Stick to your guns."

"With Lexie, you can actually see how teen moms do it, you know? Like first I thought maybe she'd be too young. Paul was worried. Seventeen! Well, eighteen now. Paul was like, let's just get a *real* nanny from a service. With experience. He goes, the au pair thing, that's for people who can't afford better. But I go, I swear, I have such a good feeling about her! And I was right! I mean. All those teen moms out there? Maybe they actually do a good job!"

"There are economic difficulties, I think. Often. Aren't there?"

"Well, yeah. And school. That's true."

A nice segue. She brought up the objective: get Paul to foot the bill for Lexie's education. At least, precollege. Just a few courses, she said. Lexie could do some of them online, while taking care of the baby. Lora nodded and enthused, now dabbing, now holding up her toenails for Aleska's approval. Their new color was a garish orange. Could stun a horse at ten paces. In good conscience, she could not praise the hue.

Lora was skilled with that nail-polish brush, she deflected. How *did* she not go over the edges?

Paul would be the stumbling block, of course. As a rule, he was only generous with himself.

After Lora left she brought up the document on her screen. *The document*, she thought. There were thousands of documents on the drive, but this one said what she wanted at her funeral. She wasn't morbid, just meticulous. One thing from the New Testament, one only, and not unusual for funerals, indeed it bordered on the hackneyed. But it was simple and she'd always been fond of simple sentiments. The missionaries had taught her the Psalms. *It is creation that turns us back to dust, saying: "Go back, oh child of earth."*

When she was younger and thought of her own funeral— rarely—she had briefly considered who might be present, which friends and colleagues, whether Jake would still be alive. Men predeceased, often. Common knowledge. The thought of the guests had been almost frivolous. No, it had been frivolous. And yes, Jake had predeceased. Died by his own hand, as they used to put it. He had always suffered, even threatened from time to time: *Selbstmord*. He preferred the German word to the Polish. More brutal. Fitting to the act, he said. An act against others. He saw it for what it was. But in the end he'd not been able to resist. The millstone was too heavy. He'd been Jake to her for decades, but was still Jakub to himself. Jakub from the camps. Who saw too much and could never forget. Never medicated, of course. Their generation wasn't given to psychopharmacology. It might have saved him, though.

She'd been shocked despite the warnings she'd had. Shocked not by the impulse, but by the lapse in his kindness. He'd been such a kind man. Small gestures of kindness, constantly. *You left me*, she'd said to the memory of him. *By choice. By choice. By choice you left me here alone.* The shock had taken years to recede. To this day she missed his face, his hands, his bearing. Broad shoulders, though he always stood a bit hunched. He always claimed to have poor posture, but she had loved the way he stood.

Almost none of them were alive, those past, future mourners. Thus: almost no mourning.

On good days, she could see it as freedom.

Last night she'd slept fitfully and woken from the dream—the dream of children, was that what it was? Terrible children. Or short people dancing in a ring—and heard Lexie talking on her phone outside. Lexie pacing in the garden, alongside the flower-beds outside the open window.

An open window onto a garden: all she needed at night. The lift of a cool breeze from an open window. Cocktails at dusk, and then a warm wind after dark. That famous poem by Eichendorff. *"Sehnsucht." Am Fenster ich einsam stand / Und horte aus weiter Ferne / Ein Posthorn im stillen Land* . . . it didn't translate well. "Yearning." *I stood alone at the window / And heard in the far distance / A horn in the peaceful country.* In drifted the fragrance of night-blooming jasmine.

On the phone Lexie had been disagreeing with someone. Or refusing to do something.

Then she'd fallen asleep again and now she wasn't sure: it might have been part of the dream, Lexie talking. Before that, the short people dancing around her, slowly swaying. But their faces were blurred, their features . . . no. Did they even have features?

They had eyes. Oh yes.

But *were* they children?

They were not.

Now she remembered. Shivered. That old tingle at the tips of her fingers, as though a sliver of glass was being drawn along beneath the nails. A thin point. Would it break the skin?

She'd been so relieved when Lexie's voice woke her. It had saved her from that dark ring. The faces with eyes burning.

She could just ask her, ask Lexie. Had she been walking in the garden. Real? Or had that been the dream?

But Lexie would think she was losing it—at her age, the default assumption. She probably was.

And here was Lexie now. She stood behind the screen door, the baby in a carrier on her front, a hand on the bottom, jiggling and patting. The baby fussed.

"Come in, dear. Come on in."

The screen banged behind her.

"Sorry. Lora just left with the personal shopper and Dolores has the afternoon off for Flavio's chemo? And now there's people at the gate. A contractor from the renovation company and some guys to service the HVAC, he said. But Lora told me not to let anyone in if I didn't already know them. She said it, like, three times. She's afraid of that deaf guy Paul's suing."

"That poor man. She's afraid of *him*?"

"I thought you could decide. If it's OK to let them in." .

"She might have forgotten the appointment. Did you text her?"

Lexie nodded, slipped her phone out of a pocket as she bounced the baby. Glanced at the screen and put it back.

"And Paul. But I haven't heard back from either of them. And the guys are just waiting."

"You could ask them to reschedule."

"But that's—I mean—there's a whole crew out there."

"Oh, hell. Let them in. I'll take responsibility if they rob us. You can blame it on the senile old lady."

Lexie smiled, looked like apology. Turned to go.

"Wait. May I ask you something?"

"Sure."

"Sometimes I don't sleep well. I can't always tell what's a dream. And I'm worried that maybe I'm losing it. My grip on so-called reality . . . so maybe you can help me. Last night or early this morning. Were you outside my window? Talking in the garden?"

Lexie looked startled. Almost guilty. Then she pulled her face together.

"Yeah. Yes. I was."

"Oh! Good. Good. So I'm not demented yet."

But Lexie stood there. Indecision.

"There's this —I have some bad stuff going on."

"Oh?"

"Yeah."

She waited. Best not to urge disclosure. Best to listen.

"This stepbrother of mine. Ely?"

"The older one. Ely and—Tosh? Was that his name?"

"Toff. Close enough. It's short for Christopher. So first off They're drug dealers."

"Oh."

"And it used to be mostly meth, but now a lot of meth comes up from Mexico so they deal pills also. But business isn't going so good. Ely lost some connections when my stepfather died? So he wants me to hook him up. With new clients. Because I'm here. You know. Living with rich people."

"Well. That's ridiculous. Paul's friends would never buy meth. And they get their pills from actual doctors. Anyway, drugs. Isn't that typically a seller's market?"

Lexie nodded, then shook her head and bounced the baby. Looked anxious.

"He's desperate, I guess. For money. And see, he has something on me. So it's like, kind of a blackmail deal."

"Good lord, Lexie. Quite a telenovela, isn't it?"

"He has some information I didn't know he had. That could, like, really hurt my mother. And he says he'll tell her. If I don't hook him up."

"Are you going to tell me? What this information is?"

"You might not want to know. Like, TMI. Honestly."

"TMI?"

"Too Much Information?"

"Go ahead, please."

"It's that. OK."

The girl's mouth twisted nervously. Her face was ashen.

"It's that my stepfather was unfaithful. And it was me. He, you know. He had sex with me. I mean. I didn't want him to. You know. But he did. And Ely knew. Knows. Whatever. I didn't know he ever saw anything. But it turns out he did."

The poor dear looked queasy. At least the baby had gone quiet. Small mercies.

"Why don't you sit down," said Aleska gently.

"I can't, she'll wake up if I do. Anyway. I've gotta let those guys in."

When the screen door had banged again she looked up at her propaganda pieces on the wall over her desk. The Stalin poster. Papa Joe holding a baby up the clouds. Lifting a bright little cherub to the sky.

What we do to our children.

She herself, what had she done? Benign neglect. Lost in the daydreams. Sometimes nightmares. The sedimentation of everyday life. Now and then, when Paul was not so small anymore, she'd caught herself forgetting he existed. For hours at a time. How old had he been then? Ten? Twelve? He would go into his room, or run around with the kids from the neighborhood. Hunkered down in a basement cave, playing video games. Later, when he was grown and gone from the rooms of her orbit, she forgot him for days. When he was small she'd been suitably attentive.

Until his needs appeared to diminish. *Appeared* was operative. For they needed so much, all of them. They needed so much forever.

It had been vital, at first, that he be sheltered, as her sister hadn't been. Only after a while it seemed to her that, living in plenty and in peace, he should be fine.

Yet he was not. There were totalitarians always ascendant. Fools and demagogues. And her son would not lift a hand against them.

He would never be in that brave legion.

There was a man at her door. Chunky. Baseball cap backward on his head. Work boots.

What time was it? Had she eaten lunch?

She didn't recall, damn it.

"Yes?"

"We'll need to turn the power off. To the main house. Not too long. Wanted to let you know."

Then he moved off. Lexie was in his place. Pushed open the screen and came in. Her face still shadowed. No baby. She held the monitor in her hand.

"She went to sleep. She's in her bassinet."

"I'll need your phone, dear."

"My phone?"

"Yes. Bring up your stepbrother's number for me. Then you can leave. No need for you to listen in. Oh. But write his full name down for me, would you? Date of birth, with the year. And his address. There. On the Post-it notes."

"But what—"

"Just let me handle it."

"Seriously?"

The phone said 3:18.

Early, yes. But the situation called for it. Needs must.

"Before you leave, pour me a drink."

Thus fortified, Lexie having bowed out, she pressed the call icon. An analog receiver: soon they'd stop using the image, no doubt. Kids could barely identify it already. By the time Lexie was her age, or Rae, herself long dead, all the symbols would be different. Or most. Would a green light still mean go, even?

She felt cold and clean. Iron Lady. Like that old Tory bulldog in England. Ran the country. Now deceased. Sometimes names failed temporarily, but the memory would return.

"Yeah?"

Drug dealers had no manners these days. Back in the sixties, when she and Jake were doing LSD, they'd had a dealer who wore an ascot. And a smoking jacket. He'd styled his hair in an Afro, with jeweled combs stuck in. He was from New York, Harlem, but spoke immaculate French.

She told the man who she was—Lexie's employer in Brentwood, she said. Technically a counterfactual statement. But no need to get into the weeds. She told him the name of her lawyer. Taking a cue from Paul. *When in doubt, lawyer up*, he liked to say. She told him of the satisfaction she would have in turning him in. For both the pharmaceutical opioids and the methamphetamines. She read off his address and DOB. She told him she was indifferent, personally, as to whether he disclosed the history of molestation to his stepmother, but for his sake she advised against it. She told him not to call Lexie again. She asked him if he had any questions. He muttered. A half-wit, apparently.

"Enunciate, please."

"Say what?"

"Speak with your mouth open, so that the sounds can pass your lips. I wish to know that you understand. If Lexie hears from you again, or if she discerns from her mother that you've spoken of these unsavory matters, your contact information will be passed along by my attorney, who already retains it, to the relevant authorities. Are we clear?"

Long pause. Something rustling. Faint, driving beat.

"Fuck. Yeah. I get it. And fuck you very much."

"Good. You may hang up now."

"You bitch."

"Indeed."

Margaret Thatcher, that was it.

If only there were more such tasks she could accomplish from her desk chair. How she missed walking! She missed that most of all. She saw people walking, ambling slowly, striding briskly, and felt a pang of the purest envy.

She was finishing off her drink when Lexie poked her head in. Still minus baby, plus monitor.

"So one of the HVAC guys put a screw through a water pipe? And then he made a worse mistake, the contractor said. He was so pissed at him? The guy drilled the screw through the pipe, and then he realized what he'd done and took it out again."

Was there a gentle way to advise her not to end declarative sentences with a question mark? Lora was worse. Yes: Point out that Lora did it. Discuss its ineffectiveness. The fact that it undermined authority. Note to self, for later conversation.

"Flooding?"

"Dirty water got on that rug Paul's so proud of. From Abu Dhabi or whatever?"

"Dubai, I believe it was."

"Yeah. The Dubai rug. He said it cost more than his car. Didn't he?"

"An exaggeration. Almost certainly."

"But still."

"I detect a fresh litigation opportunity."

"Oh, man. I'm toast."

"Don't worry, dear. It's not your responsibility. And I spoke to your stepbrother. I think he'll probably steer clear. Though I can't be sure. He's not the sharpest knife."

"Seriously? What did he say?"

"Not much."

She needed to get out. Walker or no walker.

Lexie was saying thank you. Effusive. She waved a hand. No thanks were needed. If Lexie was her keeper now, she could also be Lexie's.

"I'd like to go out," she told her. Was it too abrupt? Sometimes she spoke abruptly these days. Skipped a beat.

"Oh. OK. Should I wake up the baby?"

"No. I'll go by myself. Maybe walk around the block. I'll need help up, of course."

"All by yourself? It's no problem. I can just put her in the stroller."

"By myself. I insist."

Lexie didn't like it. She stood a minute, indecisive.

"Bring the walker over, would you please?"

Finally she was foot-borne, making her way along the garden path. The flagstones were uneven; you had to watch the walker's rubber feet didn't catch on an edge. The street would be better. Although: no sidewalk till the corner. Maybe a swiftly passing car would knock her over. She'd bounce like a bowling pin. Land on her side and roll. Her passage was so slow Lexie made circles around her as she went by the side of the house. Clearing obstacles. She moved a hose for her, opened the first gate, moved a dolly standing beside the open back doors of the workers' van. Opened the second gate and held it.

"You have your cell, right?"

She'd seen her pack it, but still needed reassurance.

Had to wear a hideous so-called fanny pack around her waist these days. Purses were no use anymore; they swung and got in the way. No surer sign of full capitulation. *I have no dignity*, the object broadcasted. *No, not a shred.*

"Right here, dear. Yes. I'll call if I have a heart attack."

"Very funny. So, so funny."

Then she was on the asphalt. Felt like a jailbreak. One of those condescending yet supposedly heartwarming films where crotchety old folk went AWOL on a day trip from a home, became carefree children again. Playing baseball or something. Running around on the grass. What would her grandson say? Busting up shit? Busting loose? Busting a nut? Not sure what that meant. Could ask him. Better not to lose face: look it up in the urban slang dictionary. Maybe she'd busted some drug-dealer nut already. Or maybe not at all.

Nice shade from the sweeping branches above. Two houses down was a humdinger, a Mediterranean-villa-crossed-with-medieval-castle atrocity. A child's idea of opulence. Turrets and crenellations combined with terracotta roof tiles. She smiled as she passed.

Jake had liked to walk, could walk for hours and never get tired. Lived in California for decades but didn't get used to cars. Fitting that he chose a car to die in, fitting that he chose gas. So many wounds that never healed. He hated the American way of thought that said all things could be repaired, all things surmounted by a trick of attitude. History is trivial in this country, he said. Forgetting is the way to bliss. Ignorance is a badge of honor.

All accurate. All known. And yet, she'd said to him. Begged, honestly, because begging was what you did when you were powerless. Look what it gives them, Jake. What it gives us, if we choose to accept the gift. They're always beginning. You begin again every day, when you have almost no memory. It's a country of phoenixes!

It's a country of dodos, he said. And look what happened to them.

She got it. One was mythological, the other simply extinct. But she'd always come down on the side of the myths.

There was satisfaction in walking, even with the awkward contraption. Manicured shrubs, tall trees, grand houses—grand in size, at least. Nobody else walking on the street. It wasn't a neighborhood for pedestrians. Wait: a young girl walking her dog. Slender and tall. The dog also. A whippet or a greyhound. Did she greet her? Did she meet her eyes? Did she think, *old lady*?

It was all she thought, probably. If she thought anything.

Cars were beginning to pull into drives, the end of work. The close of business. Nearing the cocktail hour. Here a woman in a Range Rover, a man in a Porsche. Revving, revving. Showing off its engine.

What had they done with their days? Were they proud? Or was it resignation?

She passed each house in turn, each gate, each privacy hedge or showy rock garden, but as she passed them she also passed nothing at all. They were different and the same: she moved and did not move. What was ahead was past.

Was that what it was like? When you were coming to the end?

A car beside her didn't pass. It slowed and stopped. Silver. Window came down. Silent. Paul's face. Paul's car, therefore.

"Time to get in," he said. Earbuds.

"I'm taking a walk," she said.

"People are worried about you," he said.

Did he even hear her? He might be on his phone. He might be talking to anyone.

"Lexie says you've been out here for hours. Two and a half hours now, she said."

"No, that's not true," she said.

Impossible. She'd only just got here.

"It felt like minutes," she added.

"You're going in circles," he told her, impatient. "Lexie saw you walk past the house. Three times. You've got to be getting tired. Aren't you? We should call it a night. I'll drive you home. OK?"

She leaned on the walker's handles. Turned and gazed in at him. His face was partly Jake's, of course. Partly his own face as a child, beneath the bulk and jowls.

"It's called walking around the block," she said. "There are beautiful gardens."

He looked at her. Waiting.

"I only want to keep going."

Something changed in his expression. Almost softened.

"Of course you do," he said.

They looked at each other for another moment, and then his window went up. He pulled away again.

She watched his taillights flash on as he stepped on the brakes at the stop sign, turned the corner. And then her son was gone.